Locked In

Locked In

Peter Conway

ROBERT HALE · LONDON

© Peter Conway 2006
First published in Great Britain 2006

ISBN-10: 0-7090-8194-4
ISBN-13: 978-0-7090-8194-4

Robert Hale Limited
Clerkenwell House
Clerkenwell Green
London EC1R 0HT

2 4 6 8 10 9 7 5 3 1

Typeset in 11/15pt Palatino
Printed in Great Britain by St Edmundsbury Press
Bury St Edmunds, Suffolk
Bound by Woolnough Bookbinding Limited

CHAPTER ONE

The opposing team had been camped on their twenty-five-yard line for a good ten minutes and when the referee blew his whistle for yet another set scrum following an infringement by one of his team mates, Michael Donovan took a deep breath before packing down again. Thirty-five he may have been, but he could still show the youngsters a thing or two about stamina and even if he wasn't quite as quick off the mark as he once had been, his reading of the game was such that he was able to start in the right direction a second or two before most of the others. As he lowered his shoulder to push, out of the corner of his eye, he saw the opposing fullback coming up on his right and the moment the opposition's hooker won the ball and the scrum half was committed to the pass, he set off for the corner flag. Even though he was running flat out, for a few seconds he thought that he was going to be too late, but then, at precisely the right moment, he launched himself horizontally at the opposing player. The man saw him coming, hesitated for a fatal second, half putting out his arm to hand him off, but then the two of them hurtled into touch in a tangle of arms and legs, uprooting the corner flag.

'Well tackled, Mike. You all right? Come on, old lad, one

last effort – we've only got to keep them out for another couple of minutes.'

Michael Donovan staggered back to the lineout, the world spinning crazily around him and shook his head as he saw two balls coming towards him from the long throw-in. He tried to bring his arms up to catch it, but he had no control over his muscles and was already sinking to the ground when simultaneously the ball hit him on the chest and his opposite number cannoned into him. The piercing blast of the referee's whistle and the angry protestations of the man who had grabbed the ball and had been robbed of the opportunity to score, came through to him with absolute clarity, as did the feel of the wet grass under his legs, but he was quite incapable of moving a muscle.

'Shut up and get the trainer – can't you see that he's seriously injured?'

'It's only a spot of concussion.'

'No, look at his eyes – he's blinking.'

'Do you think it's his neck?'

'It's all right, old chap, we won't move you until the ambulance men come, just to be on the safe side.'

Donovan tried desperately to speak, to tell them that he wasn't able to breathe properly, that he was drowning in his own saliva, that he was dying. But he wasn't able to move a muscle except for those in his eyelids.

'Look at his colour! Get him on to his back, quick.'

Fingers pinched his nose, he felt lips pressed on his and then air, not fresh air, but air with the taste of tobacco on it, life-giving air nonetheless, was being forced into his lungs.

The next two weeks were a sustained nightmare; there was the initial flurry of activity, the dash to the hospital, an anaesthetic, a confusion of machines, sombre conversations held just out of earshot of which he was only able to catch the odd word, and a feeling of complete impotence. To start with, his greatest fear was that they wouldn't realize that he was fully conscious, that he was able to feel everything, that they might carry out painful procedures on him, even an operation without anaesthetic. Soon, though, a comforting female voice reassured him about that, seeming to sense what he was thinking.

'Are you able to blink voluntarily? Do three for me, will you? Right, one blink for yes and two for no. Are you quite comfortable? You're not? Which part of you is hurting? Your neck? Your arms? Your legs? Your back? Right, that's probably just your position; I'll get the nurse to help me to move you.'

The woman was brisk and matter of fact and within ten minutes the situation was spelled out. He had been born with an abnormality of one of the arteries at the base of his brain and the blow he had received on the head as the result of the Rugby tackle had caused it to expand suddenly, starving the brain stem of blood and hence oxygen. For the time being he would have to have artificial respiration through a tracheotomy, be fed through the tube running up through his nose and into his stomach, and his joints kept mobile by the physiotherapists.

'Don't worry,' the woman said, just before leaving. 'We do know that you can feel everything and understand all that's going on. I'll be looking in to see you at least twice a day.'

It was true, he thought, that what she'd said had reassured him to some extent, but the two questions that really mattered and the ones that hung like a black cloud over his head were never answered. How could they be when he lacked the ability to ask them? When was he going to start recovering and how much disability was he going to be left with? The ultimate terror was that he might remain as he was, kept alive for years, a grotesque advertisement for the intensive therapy unit of St Cuthbert's Hospital.

Each day merged into the next, with him at times dozing and at others listening to the radio and iPod through earphones. Although he could see and blink, he was unable to move his eyes in any meaningful way and the inability to scan from side to side made it impossible for him to read and watching the television was an effort that was too uncomfortable to sustain for any length of time. At least, though, he could see the nurses and physiotherapists who attended to him, which made their visits less impersonal, even though, unlike the anaesthetist, they made no real effort to talk to him.

At the beginning, he looked forward to visitors with eager anticipation, but he soon began to dread their appearance. The partners in his firm, the members of his Rugby club and his other friends soon ran out of things to say; he could feel their unease and sense their disbelief that the seemingly inanimate object in front of them really was alive. Helen was the one who stuck it out the longest, but when at first she missed a day, then began to come once a week, and eventually not at all, he felt nothing but relief. Their relationship had been fun, but it had hardly scratched the surface of either of them and who could blame someone as active and physical as Helen for wanting to escape the sights and smells of the intensive therapy unit?

The one exception to his dislike and even fear of visitors was Father Carey, who appeared for the first time a few days after his admission. The word 'appeared' carried the implication, he thought, that the man had materialized, but that would have been totally misleading – in fact, he made an entrance. Donovan heard him coming, his heavy footsteps reverberating along the corridor and the hushed tones that even the doctors affected in the ITU were clearly not for him.

'And where's this fellow countryman of mine?'

'We don't know that he's Irish, Father.'

'What else could he be, Staff Nurse, with a name like Donovan, tell me that?'

The accent was pure Connemara and the face that swam into Donovan's view with its ruddy complexion was as much in keeping as his cloak and black biretta, which he doffed as he leaned over.

'You needn't look so surprised, young man,' he said. 'If you are a priest, you might as well look like one.' He paused, his eyes twinkling. 'If you don't, the magic might not work and that would never do, would it?'

He let out a loud guffaw and pressed the hand he was holding more firmly. It was the first time since the accident that anyone had acknowledged that Donovan had any thoughts, let alone divined them and straight away he felt his spirits lift a little.

'I used to play a bit myself when I was younger, but I was never any good – too fat even at that age. They tell me that you were a pillar of the London Irish a few years back; did you ever come across Con Murphy?'

Donovan hardly took in what the man was saying, just deriving comfort from the voice and the man's peculiarly Irish face, with its small twinkling eyes, which disappeared almost completely whenever he laughed, something he did all the time. The priest wasn't to know that Donovan hadn't given religion serious thought for a good fifteen years, but he had a strong suspicion that the man wouldn't have cared one jot, even if he had. What if the man's collar was none too clean, that his nails were dirty and his breath smelled strongly of whiskey? Father Carey was the first person to have treated him as if he still had a mind and feelings. It wasn't that he could fairly have taken exception to the way he was cared for by the doctors, nurses and physiotherapists, it was just that it was delivered so impersonally. Perhaps, he thought, that was the only way they could keep going and who was he to criticize when he had treated his own clients in exactly the same way? 'Don't get emotionally involved with them,' the senior partner had said when he had first joined the practice, 'it won't help them and it'll certainly be bad for you.' Had that really been true? Surely he would have served some of the pathetic people involved in messy divorce cases better if he, too, hadn't been quite so detached.

'I can see that I'm tiring you. Goodbye ·for now – I'll look in again tomorrow and we can have another little talk.'

It was uncanny how the priest always seemed to know exactly what he was thinking – no one else did. He had tried with the staff in the unit to put expression into his eyes, or even the way he blinked, but to no avail; Father Carey, though, merely had to sit by him, he would start to speak and more often than not the subject was connected with something that was either in his mind or at the back of it.

One evening – it was at about eight-thirty and the visitors of the other two patients on the ward had gone – Donovan heard the priest approaching. Since his first few days in the ITU, his skill in interpreting sounds had improved out of all recognition and he detected the unsteadiness of the man's gait immediately. The reason became obvious as soon as Father Carey sat down by his bed; Donovan had smelled the whiskey on the man's breath often enough before, but this time he was drunk. The hand that took his was shaking, the voice was unaccustomedly low and the words slurred.

'I know that you must often think that there could be nothing worse than lying here not being able to move or talk and fearing that with every passing day there is less chance of recovery, but I tell you, my friend, there is. What happened to you in the pursuit of healthy exercise must seem grossly unfair especially to someone who, I suspect, has little sense of religion, but if God does make it up to you in the next life, what about the poor soul in the isolation cubicle over there? His brain is full of maggots, rotting from the effects of the virus, which is today's plague. What do you suppose goes on in what is left of his mind, when all the human contact he has is with people dressed up like men and women from Mars? Why do they despise the poor man so much? I even heard Sister Garrard say that he deserves all he has got. I must say that she is a fine one to talk. It's easy enough to take a high and mighty attitude to temptation when you've never been tempted, but when you have and have given in to it and then go about preaching – that's what sticks in my gullet. She's not the only one, either. You might think that you are surrounded by Doctor Schweitzers and Mother Theresas, but you're not – this place is a veritable Pandora's box. Open the lid a fraction and all sorts of unpleasant things creep out.

'Now I know what you're thinking – the drunken old fool is about to break the secrets of the confessional.' The priest gave one of his chuckles. 'Well, I'm going to disappoint you. For one thing the great majority here are a

Godless lot and aren't even Catholics and, for another, those who are hardly ever come to confession. How do I know what's going on, then? I'll tell you; I spend a lot of time here; I talk to people and they talk to me. It can't have escaped your notice that the grain and grape are not strangers to my palate; well, people think that I'm just an inebriated old fool, but only half that statement is true and I know more about a lot of people here than they know themselves. Why, only the other day, I heard that....'

Michael Donovan lost track of time as the man went through practically all the people who had looked after him during his stay and told him which ones were saints, which ones pretended to be saints and were really sinners, which ones were sinners and knew it, and which ones were ordinary mortals.

'It's nothing more than a microcosm of the world at large, which is what you'd expect. And where do I stand, you might ask?' The priest shook his head. 'I'll leave that for others to judge.'

'I really think you ought to go now, Father, it's getting very late and night sister will be here soon.'

Donovan saw the man look across at the nurse and smile. 'You're quite right – it would never do to have her catching me upsetting the routine, now would it? Goodnight, Michael – I always enjoy our little chats.'

Father Carey failed to come in the following day and the one after and Donovan was left believing that the man was regretting his drunken confidences and that his visits would now be at an end. Certainly Donovan now looked at those who were involved in the running of the ITU and came into the ward during the next twenty-four hours in a completely different light. Doctor Melrose, the anaesthetist responsible for the technical side, particularly assisted respiration, Doctor Longley, the physician in charge of the unit, Sister Mountfield and even Liz and Jacquie, the nurse and physiotherapist who spent the most time with him, had all been subjects of Father Carey's dissection. The one person he hadn't mentioned, apart from oblique allusions, was Claire Garrard, the night sister. Now why was that, he wondered?

Just how much Donovan had come to depend on the priest only became apparent to him that night. He had spent most of the day looking forward to the man's visit and then when he didn't appear, doubting if he would remain sane if all the company he had was that of the doctors, nurses and physiotherapists. Jacquie, his regular physiotherapist, was an attractive, well-rounded, cheerful young woman and if he had been able to speak, he would have enjoyed a little gentle flirtation with her, but although she always asked him if she was hurting him when she moved his joints, she never talked to him properly. Quite often, in fact, she spoke to the nurse across him, almost as if he was a lump of wood, something that he found both distressing and humiliating in the extreme.

Apart from Father Carey, the only other people who did talk to him regularly were Doctor Melrose, who had explained the position originally, and Doctor Longley. Every day, sometimes twice, they came to check on his condition and asked him to attempt to move his muscles, also testing his sensation, but although he could still feel their pins and cotton wool normally, as for the rest, there was nothing, not the merest flicker of activity, apart from that in his eyelids.

Hearing the heavy tread and booming voice of Father Carey the following evening immediately brought back memories of the time in childhood when he had managed to convince himself that his father had gone for good, when in fact he had merely been away for a few days on a business trip. The relief now, as then, with the return of the man, together with his father, who meant more to him than any other, was indescribable and he felt the tears rolling down his cheeks.

'Why, Michael, I do believe you thought I'd abandoned you.'

The priest pulled a silver flask out of the hip pocket of his black trousers, uncapped it and took a healthy swig before picking a piece of gauze out of the carton on the shelf above the bed and gently dabbing Donovan's face.

'God save us, didn't Sister Garrard tell you? I had to fly back to Ireland to see my old father who's had a heart attack and I left a message for her to do so. No, I can see that she didn't. That pious young woman and I are going to have a few words. Yes, I know you'd rather I didn't, but it's about time she realized the importance of sins of omission. Does she ever talk to you? Don't answer, I know very well what she'll have said: "I'll pray for you." A fat lot of good that'll do coming from her, I can tell you.'

It was uncanny how the priest seemed to know everything. Donovan remembered the evening that Sister Garrard had come in to relieve the duty nurse for twenty minutes to give her a break and he had been half asleep at the time. He hadn't opened his eyes when he felt her fingers on the sheet, which was the only thing covering him, but then did so a fraction of a second after she had drawn it right down to the foot of the bed. All the other members of staff had treated his body as if it was just a body, but she stared at it with an expression of intense concentration and he flinched internally as she reached out to touch him, but then she withdrew her hand abruptly and pulled the sheet back up as she heard the footsteps outside.

'So sad in someone so young,' she said in deathbed tones, as she was leaving. 'I'll pray for him, Nurse Thompson.'

The nurse, a comfortable married woman, who did occasional night duty to supplement the family income, had not been impressed.

'Sanctimonious bitch,' she had said under her breath when the other woman had gone, and he could still hear her muttering to herself as she checked the connections on the respirator.

It was a day or two later and Donovan was dozing when he was suddenly woken by the priest's voice.

'Now, Michael, pay attention. You're not to go to sleep on me – I've got some important news for you. I've decided that it's about time you had a change of scenery – you'd like that, wouldn't you?'

Would he like it? Donovan blinked once and then after a pause, did so again.

'What I'm going to suggest isn't that exciting, you know, but I've managed to persuade Doctor Melrose to bring you down to the chapel on Sunday at ten o'clock for Mass and Holy Communion. Yes, I know you haven't been to confession for more years than you'd care to remember, but most people just go through the motions anyway, except some I could mention, but won't. We'll just run through a list and you can tell me if there's anything you'd like to get off your chest – you might find it a comfort, a lot of people do. Now, don't go worrying about Doctor Melrose – she thinks it's a grand idea and would like to be there just to see that you come to no harm. They'll use a portable respirator to bring you down and keep you comfortable during Mass. I

had in mind a short address as I have something important to say, but I promise you that it won't be too long and
I won't embarrass you by talking about you. You didn't
think they'd have a Catholic chapel in a heathen place like
this, did you?' He gave another of his great guffaws. 'Well,
they don't – it's one of these multi-denominational places,
in its time blessed by every bishop of every faith in the
diocese. And don't think you'll get the pap of the vernac-
ular mass – I'm a covert follower of Cardinal Lefebre.
Latin and tradition is what most people want and that's
what they're going to get from me, however much the
local hierarchy may disapprove. Anyway, the proof of the
pudding's in the eating and that place'll be full, mark my
words.'

Donovan had not found himself looking forward to
anything as much since he was a child. Even Doctor
Melrose, who normally seemed devoid of any spark of
frivolity, seemed positively skittish that morning.

'I can't imagine why I didn't think of it myself,' she said.
'You must be bored to distraction with watching TV,
listening to the radio and staring up at the ceiling. I'm
even looking forward to it myself. Do you know, I haven't
been to church for ten years and, but for you, I don't
suppose I'd have had anything to do with it again unless,
of course, some interfering relative decided that I needed
some help after my death. I even told Father Carey once
that it was all a lot of twaddle, but you can't get him to rise
to a remark like that – not like Mr Calvert. All he did was
give a great laugh and said, "If it is a lot of twaddle, all I've
been doing is wasting a lot of my time, but if it isn't, I'm
not sure I'd want to be in your shoes." '

It was by far the longest speech that Donovan had ever
heard her make and, as she leaned over him to change the

connection of the tracheotomy set to link him to the portable respirator, he saw that she had a faint flush on her normally pale cheeks. Perhaps, he thought, she wasn't quite the mechanical humourless person he had assumed her to be.

Surely, he thought, as one after another, all the staff looking after him came up to him in the chapel, they couldn't all be Catholics. It was only then, when he realized how ridiculous he was being and that that wasn't the reason, that the emotion of the occasion got to him and the tears began to flow again. As on the previous occasion, it was Father Carey who noticed and lowered the temperature with a joke.

'I'd better leave this in your safe keeping,' he said, fishing the whiskey flask out of his hip pocket. 'Old Father O'Laoghaire caught me saying Mass with it on me once and I thought I'd never hear the last of it. I usually leave it in the vestry, but there are so many people around today that you never know who might slip in there and take it. I'll hide it behind the flower vase just there on the table behind you and don't be letting anyone sneak off with it, will you?' He gave Donovan a wink. 'I'm just off to change now. You'll be taking Holy Communion, won't you? Don't be worrying now, I'll come to you first and just touch the host to your lips.'

In many ways, Donovan wished that the doctors and nurses had been a little less attentive. Throughout the Mass, if it wasn't Doctor Melrose fiddling with the respirator, it was Doctor Langley feeling his pulse and, not to be outdone, the registrar, Doctor Pentland, taking his blood pressure. He couldn't help thinking, either, that the reason for there being three nurses nearby, Sister Mountfield, Sister Garrard and Liz Farmer, was a good deal more to do with keeping up appearances than for any medical need.

Donovan sensed by the sudden silence that Father Carey had come out of the vestry, then he felt the priest brush past him and in the angled mirror above his head, which had been adjusted so that he was able to see the altar, the man came into view. He looked magnificent in his robes and during his address; gone was the jocular, hard-drinking and worldly priest and in his place was the dignified hospital chaplain who had something serious to say.

'It has always been the vocation of doctors, nurses and paramedical staff to look after the sick and dying and the medical profession is a noble calling, but there have been times in its history when its reputation has become tarnished. Doctors have been involved in torture and even in experimentation on prisoners and nurses have assisted them, but you may say, all this has happened in other countries and in other cultures. That may be true, but I did not think that I would live to see the day when I heard sick souls humiliated and blamed for their illness and treated as if they were less than human. Are smokers with lung cancer and drinkers with cirrhosis of the liver told that they have brought these illnesses on themselves and that they deserve the fate that has overtaken them? Of course they're not – I'm quite sure that the very thought is repugnant to you. In that case, why is that very thing done to AIDS victims? To be charitable, one may say that fear is a factor, but when did fear stop doctors and nurses looking after those with plague, tuberculosis and hepatitis, all more infectious maladies? The name of the Holy Father himself has been used to justify condemnation of homosexuals, but he was merely pointing out that such an unnatural practice was a sin, as adultery and theft are sins.' He paused dramatically and looked round the congregation. 'He was not saying that sinners should be shunned, that they should not be cared for and that they should not be given the opportunity to repent. Let nobody here condemn those poor souls, let us feel compassion for them and do all in our power to ease their suffering.'

The address may have been short, but that had not reduced its impact; increased it rather. Donovan may only have been able to see the altar, but his illness had made his other senses far more acute and he had heard the hiss of a sharply intaken breath, the almost imperceptible movement of someone behind him and the sudden squeak of a chair on the stone floor as the priest was speaking. There had been smells, too, the wafts of incense coming from the altar, the perfume that Liz had put on – she normally smelled of soap – and someone had been rather too free with the after-shave lotion. It had been an extraordinary experience, as had Holy Communion when Father Carey had come to him first, adjusted the mirror and said the words with such transparent sincerity that for the first time in Donovan's life they really meant something to him.

'*Corpus domini nostri Jesu Christi custodiat animam tuam in vitam aeternam,* amen.'

He felt the host just touch his lips, saw the hint of the familiar smile and experienced an extraordinary glow that went right through him. Was there really something in it after all, or was it just his reaction to all the emotion? All he did know was that for the rest of the day, he felt at peace and somehow changed by the experience. Why, though, had Father Carey not come to see him that evening or the next day? He discovered the answer to that when the priest reappeared on the Tuesday evening.

'Sorry I had to abandon you yesterday, Michael, but on Sunday night I had the most terrible attack of the runs – you never saw the like of it. It eased up yesterday, but to tell you the truth, I'm still not feeling up to much. Still, it makes one realize what a lot of the poor devils in the cancer ward here have to put up with. Chemotherapy may work for some, but can you imagine being sick for day after day for weeks on end? It doesn't bear thinking about.'

The priest did look pale and wan and Donovan noticed that his hand, which was normally warm and dry, was cold and clammy, and it was no surprise to him when, after ten minutes, Father Carey excused himself, passing his hand across his forehead.

'It wouldn't do to disgrace myself in here of all places,' he said as he got up to leave. 'I'll try to spend more time with you tomorrow.'

Donovan was half expecting the priest to fail to put in an appearance the following day and wasn't even unduly concerned about it on the one after, but when the weekend came round and there was still no sign of him, he really became worried. He heard the news on the Saturday when the day nurse went off duty and was chatting to her relief.

'Not dead? Not Father Carey! How terrible! What was it? A heart attack?'

'I don't know. He was admitted to St Gregory's and I heard a rumour that....'

The voices drifted out of earshot, but in any case, Donovan wasn't listening any more; he was too shattered to concentrate on anything other than the fact that his prop, the only person who had given him the will to go on living, had gone forever. He willed himself to die, willed it with all the power he was able to sum up, but the next day the infernal pump was still filling his lungs with air, his heart was still beating as strongly as ever, they still went on pouring nutrients down the tube into his stomach and there was nothing he could do about any of it.

CHAPTER TWO

Arthur Prescott pottered along the corridor in his carpet slippers and stooped to pick up *The Times*, which was lying on the carpet by the front door, muttering something angrily to himself as one of the sections fell out as he straightened up.

'The wretched thing's not been the same since some idiot ordained that it should become a tabloid,' he said, waving it at the young woman who had just come hurrying out of the bathroom, 'and look at this. The newsagent's gone to pieces ever since those Asians took it over. Old Mr Sparrow never did anything so crass as to staple the account to the paper – inventions of the devil, staplers, and I distinctly remember asking you to speak to them about it last month. The wretched thing's gone through two sections and I'll never be able to remove it without tearing either the pages, or my nails, and you know how I like to keep everything neat and tidy.'

Sarah was not in the best of tempers; she had made the fatal decision to lie in bed for a few minutes after the alarm had woken her and had then come to with a start to find that a further quarter of an hour had gone by. As a result, she had to do everything in more than her customary hurry and now it looked as if she was going to be late for work.

'Here, let me have it. I'll get it out with my nail file.'

Her father was still muttering to himself as she handed the paper back. 'There, good as new.'

'You will speak to them again, won't you, Sarah?'

'Yes, of course, Father. Now, I must fly. Your lunch is in the fridge and I should be back in good time this evening.'

She gave him a quick kiss on the cheek and as she closed the front door, she saw that he was already engrossed in the sports section.

Sarah Prescott arrived at the Yard feeling hot and sticky and, unusually for her, in a thoroughly bad mood. Having overslept, she had had to forego her customary shower, the underground had been more than usually crowded and there was the prospect of having to endure yet another day working for Terry Painter. How the man had ever achieved promotion to the rank of inspector was a complete mystery to her; he was the original MCP, being a short, chunky, aggressive man, who was frequently foul-mouthed. If Sarah disliked the way her father talked about Asians, always with the maximum possible stress on the first syllable, she hated Painter for his constant racist and sexist comments. He obviously resented the fact that women had established themselves in the CID and was always needling her, hardly letting her escape from the office and invariably giving her the most trivial and boring jobs. If ever she was rash enough to rise to the bait and object to anything he said, he would come back with some crushing remark, or make a coarse comment about the time of the month. It didn't help at all to realize, when she looked at her flushed and angry face in the mirror of the cloakroom along the corridor from Painter's office, that on this occasion he would have been right.

The relief at finding that the man was not expected in until later in the morning did a good deal to lighten her state of mind and she settled down to finish a report that she had started the previous day. Try as she might, though, she was quite unable to concentrate on it. How much longer was she going to be able to put up with a job that at the moment she frankly detested? It had all seemed so exciting and full of promise during her training, but now, nearly nine months of dull office routine with no opportunity to show any initiative had sapped most, if not all of her enthusiasm. At least, she thought, regular hours made looking after her father that much easier, but that was something else that— The telephone on her desk rang, sharply cutting off her uncomfortable thoughts.

'Inspector Painter's office, Sarah Prescott speaking.'

'Good morning. You're just the person I was after. This is Chief Inspector Tyrrell. Would you be free to come up to my office a little later on, say about eleven? There is something I would like to discuss with you.'

'Yes, sir, I think so, but perhaps I'd better check with Inspector Painter first.'

There was a short, but nonetheless perceptible pause before the man spoke again. 'I don't think you need worry about that. See you at eleven, then.'

Sarah put down the receiver with a thoughtful frown on her face. Although Roger Tyrrell was head of her section and several others besides, she had hardly spoken to him. He had the reputation for being unfailingly courteous, but his cultured accent and university degree was the subject of constant ribald comments, not least from Painter, who invariably put on a la-di-da voice when referring to him and accentuating his own South London accent when speaking to him directly. Why on earth, though, should the man want to see her? Sarah had no time to speculate further; the report was only half finished and it was already after ten.

As luck would have it, Painter was standing talking to his secretary when she came out of the inner office.

'Where do you think you're going?'

'Chief Inspector Tyrrell has asked to see me.'

'I seem to remember telling you that I wanted that report by eleven.'

'I've got it here, ' Sarah said, handing him the plain buff folder.

'Oh you have, have you?' he replied, almost snatching it out of her hand. 'And what does that smooth bugger upstairs want with a humble DC?'

'What that smooth bugger wants is none of your business, Painter.'

It was not all that often that Sarah had seen anyone's jaw drop open and certainly not Painter's, but it did when he whirled round to see the tall figure of Roger Tyrrell standing at the door.

'Are you ready now, Sarah? I know I'm a few minutes early, but I was on my way down from Commander Maskell's office and I thought I'd look in on the off chance.'

'Yes, of course, sir.'

Tyrrell held the door open for her and then turned to face the man who was staring at them both with an expression of open aggression on his face.

'Oh, by the way, Painter, the Commander wants to see you – at once.'

Looking back through the door, Sarah saw the man flushing angrily and she caught the secretary's eye, who gave her a conspiratorial wink in reply.

'Cup of coffee?' Tyrrell asked when they were in his office.

'Yes, please.'

So brainwashed had she become by Painter, who in similar circumstances would have had a cup without inviting her to join him and what's more, would have ordered her to get it for him, that she was scarcely able to believe her eyes when the detective went into the kitchenette and came back a few minutes later with two cups and a couple of chocolate biscuits.

Sarah took a sip of her drink and then nodded her appreciation. 'Delicious,' she said, 'I'd almost forgotten how good the genuine article is; it's been a choice of instant or canteen for the last few months and that if I've been lucky.'

'I have a friend who works at the Aliens' office in Holborn and he keeps me supplied from an excellent shop nearby.'

Tyrrell took a bite out of his biscuit and looked at her from across the desk with his level grey eyes.

'Now, to business. I can't guarantee that anything will come of this, but William Tredgold, the forensic pathologist, has got something he wants to discuss with me. He wouldn't go into details over the phone, but, knowing him, it's bound to be something interesting and unusual.'

'Where do I come in?' Sarah asked.

'Maskell has decided that it's time for a reshuffle and you've been in that office downstairs for long enough. You need some experience on the ground and my usual assistant has broken his leg.'

'Not Sergeant Bristow?'

'Yes, he was run down by a car last night. He's all right in himself, I'm glad to say, but I gather it's going to mean plaster for the next three months and he'll be out of commission for a lot longer than that.'

'I'm sorry to hear that – poor man.'

Sarah was genuinely so; she liked the comfortable, middle-aged Bristow, but even so, all that mattered to her at that moment was the knowledge that at least for the time being she would be free from the wretched bully who had made her working life so miserable. She fondly imagined that she had kept the expression of delight off her face and in any case at that moment Tyrrell seemed wholly occupied in stirring his coffee, but his next remark made it quite clear that he had noticed.

'Before you get too excited,' he said, 'I should warn you that there are a couple of snags. Firstly, there may be nothing in it, and secondly, you are going to have to meet our friend Tredgold this afternoon. You haven't had that pleasure yet, have you?'

'No, but I have heard about him and I did attend his lectures.'

'Well, in that case I don't need to warn you that his sense of humour became fixed at one of the murkier and most infantile of the Freudian levels and he particularly enjoys embarrassing women, not least his secretary, who has the appropriate, if macabre, name of Tombs.'

Sarah was about to say that she had had plenty of experience in dealing with that sort of thing at the hands of Terry Painter, but thought better of it and, in any case, at that moment the telephone rang.

'Just a moment,' he said, then put his hand over the receiver and looked up. 'Our appointment's at two, meet me here at one-thirty, would you?'

Sarah's memory of Doctor Tredgold had been of a small, quick-moving man, balding, with a neatly brushed rim of grey hair and half-moon spectacles, who had a loud, abrasive voice, which he used to good effect in his lectures. He seemed to delight in slides which had clearly been designed to shock, as had his anecdotes and his way of asking questions of the members of the class. With unerring skill, he always managed to pick on the person most likely to blush or be embarrassed by his remarks and, she remembered, it had almost invariably been one of the women, although she had herself had the good fortune to escape his attentions. She had an instinct that there would be no way of doing so on this occasion, seeing the glint in his eye when the two of them were shown into his room by his secretary, a painfully thin, diffident-looking woman, who gave a visible start at the shout of 'Enter', which followed her tentative knock on the door of his office.

'Ah, Tyrrell,' the man said, getting up from his chair, 'it is some time since I had the pleasure of a visit from you. Keeping well, I trust?'

'Yes, thank you. May I introduce my assistant, DC Prescott.'

'Your assistant?' he said with heavy emphasis on the word, looking her up and down. 'My dear young lady, you are welcome, welcome indeed. A chair, Miss Tombs, no, two chairs for our visitors. Not that one, woman, it's got the reprints on it and you know how I dislike them getting out of order.'

The man sighed loudly as his secretary scuttled around, trying to create enough space amongst the piles of books, folders and microscope slides, which were scattered all over the floor, to allow them to sit down.

'I can put up with a lack of female pulchritude around here, but when that is combined with total lack of organization, one's spirits do droop at times. I can't imagine that drooping of the spirits, or of anything else for that matter, is a problem for you, my dear Tyrrell.'

He gave Sarah a pointed look over the top of his glasses and she felt the blush just beginning to rise up her neck when Miss Tombs brushed against a pile of books perched on the edge of the desk, spilling them towards the pathologist and one of them falling into his lap. By the time they had been retrieved and he had delivered a further torrent of criticism at her, Sarah had control of herself and could hardly believe her eyes when, as the woman left the room, the ghost of a smile crossed her lips and her right eyelid twitched in the suspicion of a wink.

'Enough of this frippery,' Tredgold said, opening the file in front of him and extracting some papers. 'A Roman Catholic priest by the name of Patrick Carey was found in a coma by his housekeeper, a widow who lives across the road from the presbytery and who evidently used to go in every day to do the housework and prepare his evening meal. The man was admitted to St Gregory's Hospital and died there thirty-six hours later. It appears that a few days before, he had suffered from a sharp attack of diarrhoea and vomiting from which he seemed to make a good recovery, even being able to get back to work. Now, what raised the suspicions of the worthy Jepson at St Gregory's?' Tredgold gave a snort. 'I need hardly tell you that the answer is nothing; the man is a dunderhead and he would happily have let it pass as a case of acute hepatic necrosis secondary to a virus infection. Fortunately, though, I have been doing some research into that topic with Fletcher, the liver expert, and that is how I came to do the autopsy. The reason for doing the research is partly connected with the transplant service, but we also have an interest in Hepatitis B and some of the strange disorders that occur with AIDS.'

'And in this case?'

'Patience, my dear Tyrrell, patience; all will soon be revealed. Even Roman Catholic priests are not immune from unpleasant diseases, but the antibody tests for both AIDS and Hepatitis B were negative and there were no post-mortem signs of homosexual behaviour. Anything else occur to you?'

'Well, there's always alcohol, but I can't believe that you would have summoned us here for something as simple as that and I imagine that there are poisons that attack the liver.'

The pathologist looked distinctly disappointed. 'I was forgetting that there are some members of your profession with a reasonable endowment of grey matter. Yes, my dear fellow, you are right. The Irish as a whole and the priest-hood in particular are not averse to the doubtful pleasures of the bottle, but that was not the answer. Miss Tombs!'

The man's bellow took Sarah completely by surprise and she gave a start, which the pathologist noted, his face creasing into a vulpine grin.

'Miss Tombs, the slide projector, if you please, and a little less light.'

Tredgold waited while the woman lowered the Venetian blinds, pulled up the screen and switched on the projector.

'You are the resident botanical expert, Miss Tombs, what is your opinion about that?' he asked as the first slide came into view.

'It's a toadstool, Doctor Tredgold.'

'Even my mother, who is eighty and half blind with cataracts, not to mention the fact that she doesn't know what day of the week it is, could tell me that. What sort of toadstool, Miss Tombs?'

'I think it's a death cap, Doctor Tredgold.'

'And what leads you to that conclusion?'

'The yellowish green cap and the smooth white stem.'

'What a mine of information you are, to be sure. Does your knowledge spread to its botanical name?'

'No, sir.'

'It's *amanita phalloides*. That surely must mean something to you.'

'I'm afraid not, sir. I never was any good at Latin.'

Tredgold sighed. 'Even less so at Greek, it would appear. *Amanita* is the Greek word for fungus and your failure to know that I can understand, but are you not even aware what *phalloides* means? Stupid question, there is no way you could possibly do so. Miss Prescott, perhaps you could help us.'

'It's because that toadstool has some resemblance to the little thing that men seem so proud of.'

Tredgold let out a great bellow of laughter. 'Well said, I like "the some resemblance" bit and I agree with you. The rather sickly green colour of the cap and the white stem, though, are not wholly appropriate. I see you look mystified, Miss Tombs. Might I suggest a woman to woman tête-à-tête a little later on – you might learn something interesting.'

'What put you on to toadstool poisoning?' Tyrrell asked.

'The combination of the gastro-intestinal upset followed by hepatic and renal tubular necrosis. There aren't all that many agents that produce that particular combination of lesions and there is a radio-immune assay test for the amatoxin, which is responsible for the fatal liver and kidney damage. I found the toxin in both the blood and the urine.'

'So, there's no doubt?'

'None at all.'

'How many toadstools would constitute a fatal dose?'

'One large one.'

'And what makes you think that it wasn't an accident? This is, after all, the season for toadstools and I gather that *amanita phalloides* is common enough in this country.'

'So it is, my dear Tyrrell, but does a priest, whose beat is central London, go collecting toadstools of the deadly poisonous variety and then eat them, thinking they were mushrooms?'

'Perhaps his housekeeper picked them and gave them to him as a treat,' Sarah said.

'Some treat, but you may have a point. Nonetheless, I thought the circumstances were sufficiently unusual to draw them to your attention. As to whether it was an accident or a deliberate act either of the priest himself, or someone who wished him ill, I'll leave in your capable hands, my dear Tyrrell, not to forget those of your charming assistant. Don't neglect to have that little chat with Miss Tombs before you go, will you, my dear? I'm afraid it's a little late for her to profit from the fruits of your no doubt considerable experience, but miracles can happen, at least they could in the less cynical times of my youth. Now, and giving further thought to the character of my secretary, I'm not so sure. Well, I have work to do. Be sure to keep me informed of what, if anything, you discover.'

Miss Tombs gave Sarah a shy smile as she showed the two detectives out after having given them the address of the presbytery.

'You mustn't mind Doctor Tredgold,' she said, 'he likes his little jokes.'

Sarah waited until they were back in the car and then turned towards her superior, letting out her breath in a long sigh.

'Little jokes! Is he always like that?'

'You mean the Laurel and Hardy act with his secretary?' Sarah nodded.

'Yes, is the answer and I stopped feeling sorry for her months ago; I believe she enjoys it almost as much as he does. Incidentally, you made quite a hit with him.'

'Me? A hit?'

'Yes. The last female assistant I took to see him was reduced to tears within the first five minutes. You gave him as good as you got – he likes that. Enough of Tredgold, we'd better see what we can find out about Father Carey.'

The presbytery of the Sacred Heart was a dirty, redbrick Victorian house directly opposite the church. The small front garden might have been distinguished by that name sixty years earlier, but was now a tangle of weeds, brambles and stunted bushes, which were decorated by pieces of paper, beer cans and other assorted rubbish. The wooden gate was leaning over at an angle and, as Tyrrell lifted it up, a tabby cat appeared and rubbed itself against his trouser leg. The detective bent down to tickle it behind its one good ear, the other having had a piece taken out of it in some past fight, then straightened up and walked across to one of the dirty windows on the ground floor.

'Not exactly the height of prosperity, is it?'

Tyrrell cleared a small area in one of the panes of glass with a piece of newspaper and peered in.

'And what do you think you're doing?'

The tiny woman – she was well under five feet tall – was

wrestling ineffectually with the gate and the detective went back along the path to help her.

'You must be Father Carey's housekeeper.'

'What if I am?'

'It's Mrs?'

'Mrs Flynn.'

The accent was as thick as a glass of Baileys and the aroma about her strongly suggested that she had recently been fortifying herself either with that excellent liqueur, or something similar.

'I'm very pleased to see you. My name is Tyrrell, Chief Inspector Tyrrell, and this is my assistant Sarah Prescott; we're enquiring into Father Carey's death.'

The woman peered suspiciously at the detective's warrant card, but then, seemingly reassured by Sarah's presence, reached into the pocket of her overall.

'You'd better come in.'

While the woman busied herself by getting them a cup of tea, Tyrrell wandered around the living-room, looking at the row of books on the shelf on the wall, the worn carpet and the two easy chairs, both of which had seen better days.

'Was Father Carey a keen player?' he asked the woman when she returned with the tea tray, idly moving the one remaining white knight on the chessboard, which was sitting on an occasional table.

The woman put the tray down on the large desk set against the opposite wall and came across to where he was standing.

'It was more than my life's worth to move any of those pieces – he liked doing problems.'

'Did he ever play with anyone else?'

'He had a regular game each Thursday evening with Mr

Calvert – I'd cook supper for them and they'd settle down to it afterwards.'

'Mr Calvert?'

The woman gave a disapproving sniff. 'He's the Protestant chaplain from St Cuthbert's up the road.'

'Did Father Carey visit the hospital as well?'

'If you ask me, he spent too much time up there. I was saying to Mrs O'Shea only the other day that it wasn't like that when Father O'Malley and Father Coughlin were here.' The woman finished pouring out the third cup and looked up suspiciously. 'And?'

'We don't have any details of Father Carey's next of kin and naturally we're anxious to inform them about what's happened – we thought you might be able to help.'

Some of the suspicion went out of the woman's expression. 'I wouldn't know about that – he wasn't one to talk about his family. You might ask Mr Calvert.'

'Perhaps if I were to look through his papers, I might find a letter or something.'

'You might.'

The woman picked up her cup and, as she walked towards the door, Tyrrell gave Sarah a nod and she immediately got up and followed her into the kitchen. The detective turned towards the desk with a grunt of satisfaction; what a relief it was, he thought, to be working with someone who was quick on the uptake. So far, he had been rather impressed by Sarah – surely Maskell's doubts were unjustified.

His search of the drawers proved singularly unrewarding. Only the top central one was unlocked and the contents merely consisted of an untidy mixture of paperclips, rubber bands, dried out ballpoint pens and assorted pieces of stationery. The bookcase contained volumes more or less equally distributed between theological and medical texts and books on chess theory, but more interesting than that was the thick folder tucked into the newspaper rack by the side of the music centre. It was crammed full of cuttings from newspapers and magazines, together with reprints from medical journals, all on the same subject: AIDS. There were also notes in untidy handwriting, which looked like the basis for an article, or perhaps, he thought, more likely a sermon.

When there was no sign of Sarah returning, Tyrrell picked up a slim volume of biographies of famous chess players from off the shelf and he was about to open it when the top of a sheet of paper, which was sticking out of a massive American textbook of medicine, caught his eye. He spread it out and began to read the short paragraph written in the same hand as the other notes.

Locked in, perhaps that's not such a bad definition. What must it be like to be trapped within a body which can do nothing but blink? Accept it, I suppose, or else go mad. And Michael's not mad, not by a long chalk. It's quite remarkable what he can get into those blinks; it's almost as if we have a real conversation. Have I told him too much in all the hours I've been with him? The answer to that is that I don't know – the demon drink – but even if I have, it doesn't matter, it'll be safe with him. He's not going to get better, whatever that pompous ass Longley says, not after six months. If I were Michael, I would want to end it, even though the thought of what might be in store for me if I were to do so terrifies me, but the poor fellow won't even be able to achieve that.

The writing was even more untidy than that of the notes in the folder and the detective had the greatest difficulty in deciphering it; it was also shaky and in places the ink had run where drops of liquid had been spilt on it. Tyrrell folded the piece of paper carefully, put it into his wallet and then turned his attention to the article, which started near the top of the page where the marker had been. He found it difficult to follow and was reading it for a second time when Sarah came back into the room with Mrs Flynn. Tyrrell looked up and closed the book with a snap.

'Nothing much here, I'm afraid; most of the drawers are locked. Let's have a quick look at the other rooms.'

It didn't take them long. The dining room on the ground floor didn't look as if it had been used for years, the air inside it being stale and musty, and certainly the sparse furniture hadn't had the benefit of a dusting for many a month. As had been the case with the desk in the living room, all the drawers of the sideboard were locked, and the same was true of the bedside table in the one occupied bedroom upstairs.

'Was Father Carey in bed when you sent for the ambulance?'

'Indeed he was and you've never seen such a mess. I had to burn the sheets and the under blanket.'

'So all his clothes should be here?'

'He'd left his shirt and underwear on the chair and I took them away to wash.'

'What about his suit?'

The woman shrugged her shoulders and after trying the door of the wardrobe, which was also locked, Tyrrell went back across the room to face her.

'Right, Mrs Flynn, thank you for your help. We'll just make sure that the gas and electricity are turned off and then if you'd be good enough to let me have your key.'

'I'll do no such thing,' she said, her whole body bristling

with outrage. 'I've looked after this place for more than twenty years and—'

'And very well you have done it, I have no doubt. We will, though, have to look through Father Carey's effects in greater detail and, apart from that, the Church authorities will be worried about squatters coming in now that the house is bound to be unoccupied for some time and that means that it will have to be secured properly.' The detective paused and fixed her with an unblinking stare. 'I take it that you'd like to keep this job.'

The woman held his gaze for a few moments and then reached into the pocket of her overall, threw the key on to the bed and disappeared through the door, muttering under her breath. Tyrrell went across to the window and watched her cross the road and then turned to Sarah with a smile.

'With her around no wonder he kept everything locked up.'

'But where are the keys?'

'I think it would be best if we left that to Pocock. I don't suppose you've met him yet – he's head of the scene-of-the-crime team that works with me – but I don't think it's necessary to call in the whole lot of them. I'll give him a ring in a moment. You were a long time with that old dragon – did you find out anything of interest?'

'Just that the good Father Carey didn't like mushrooms.'

'Good grief, how on earth did you manage to get round to that particular subject?'

'It wasn't that difficult. I just said that with my job I hardly ever got the opportunity to cook and that was enough to get her talking about the good old days when there were four priests here and they knew what it was to enjoy a good Irish breakfast and a proper evening meal.

She didn't appear to have liked Father Carey over much;
he wouldn't discuss things with her like his predecessor,
which I took to mean gossiping, was for ever finding fault
about this and that and was pernickety about his food. He
wouldn't eat a cooked breakfast and didn't even appreciate the special suppers she used to prepare for him and
the chaplain from St Cuthbert's. That's when I managed to
get the subject round to casseroles and Irish stew and
slipped in a question about mushrooms. Evidently he was
extremely fussy about vegetables and wouldn't touch
mushrooms, parsnips, swedes or turnips. Those Thursday
evenings were another thing she disapproved of.'

'Why was that?'

'The idea of Rome fraternizing with the opposition
wasn't to her liking at all.'

'That I can well believe. You did a very good job there,
Sarah, and when we've seen what Jack Pocock comes up
with, I think that a visit to this Mr Calvert at St Cuthbert's
would be in order.'

CHAPTER THREE

Jack Pocock was a tall, lugubrious man in his early forties, who had an irritating habit of sniffing loudly every few seconds, which was hardly surprising, Tyrrell thought, considering that the man's shapeless dark suit, which looked as if it hadn't been cleaned since he had bought it, had a peculiarly unpleasant smell, a mixture of strange chemicals and stale sweat. Despite his unsavoury personal habits, though, people tolerated him because he was supremely good at his job. If there was anything unusual about a locality, he would notice it, anything hidden, he would find it, and the whole operation was invariably carried out neatly and quickly. Another thing that Tyrrell appreciated was that he never disturbed anything until the investigating officer had seen it *in situ*.

'Find the keys, Jack?' he asked, when the man appeared at the kitchen door in a surprisingly short time.

'Yes. The one to the wardrobe was sitting out of sight on top of it and that of the wall safe, where I found the rest of them, was in the pocket of his black suit.'

Tyrrell knew better than to praise the man for something that he would certainly consider unworthy even of comment and the two of them followed him into the dining-room where he lifted down the heavy mirror, which was hanging on a hook on the wall over the fire-place, and pointed to the safe behind it.

'Company that manufactured it has only been in business for five years,' he said, stepping back.

'I see and from its position, it must stick into the chimney.'

'Yes and that's how they managed to accommodate such a large one.'

Tyrrell turned the key and swung the door open. The base of the safe was just above eye level and he reached inside, lifting out a collection of half-a-dozen keys on a ring, followed by a neat pile of documents, done up with a length of ribbon, and finally a wallet.

'Anything of interest in these?'

'A will in favour of his two nephews, a building society passbook and some letters and photographs.'

'Is that all?'

'There's something else right at the back and with your height you should be able to reach it.'

The detective shook his head in disbelief as he opened the cardboard box and then handed it across to Sarah.

'Anything in the house to suggest that he's had a woman here?'

'Condoms aren't only used by heterosexuals these days,' Pocock said lugubriously. 'You might care to look at the photographs in the wallet.'

After Tyrrell had given her the pile of digital prints and she had studied them briefly, Sarah couldn't help thinking how naturally he handled that sort of thing. Terry Painter would almost certainly never have shown them to her in the first place, making some sarcastic comment about the adverse effect of female sensibilities on work in the police force, or if he had, would have used the opportunity to inflict the maximum possible amount of embarrassment on her.

'They were taken in the living-room; do you see the pattern of the wallpaper?'

'Well spotted, I must confess that my eyes were focused elsewhere. Did you find the digital camera, Jack?'

'In the sideboard.'

After they had looked in the various locked cupboards and drawers, Pocock gave Tyrrell a list of the contents of each of them on sheets of paper in his neat handwriting.

'Can you spare them? I'll be wanting your written report in due course.'

'Miracles of modern science – portable photocopiers are part of the gear these days.'

Tyrrell looked at his watch. 'Good work. You will let me have a full report, won't you?'

'It'll be on your desk tomorrow morning. Let me know if you decide to get the team to give it the full works.'

'Thanks, but I doubt if that will be necessary.'

After Pocock had gone, he studied the man's notes, passing each sheet across to Sarah when he had finished with it.

'Strong sex drive can be a most destructive thing, particularly for someone like Carey who has taken vows of celibacy, not to mention the direction of his interests in that way,' Tyrrell said when they had both finished reading the list of objects Pocock had found.

'Poor fellow,' Sarah replied. 'Under his particular circumstances he must have been tortured by guilt. Do you think that he and the chaplain got up to more than just playing chess?'

'It's obviously possible, but he wasn't featured in any of the photographs; all those in them were quite young, no more than late teenagers, I'd say.'

'That's true and all those SM magazines featured young boys. How on earth did Pocock know where to look for them?'

'There isn't a hiding place that he hasn't seen before and the side panel of a bath is not only easy to unscrew, but would also have been safe from Mrs Flynn's prying eyes and have provided enough space for all his gear.'

'I somehow can't see a hospital chaplain being on the receiving end of that sort of game.'

Tyrrell laughed. 'Any more than I would have imagined a Catholic priest dishing it out. You're probably right, though; the sort of young man who's prepared to co-operate with that sort of thing is more often than not a drug addict.'

'But where do you suppose Father Carey got the money from?'

'That's a good question. There were nearly fifteen hundred pounds in that wallet and he also had a building society account with a very great deal more than that in it than I, at any rate, would have expected.'

'How much?'

'Not far short of fifty thousand.'

Sarah let out a low whistle.

'And he was also fond of the whiskey; Pocock found enough Baileys and Black Bush to keep a team of navvies happy for a month.'

'None of this fits in particularly well with toadstool poisoning, does it?'

'No, it doesn't. It's not all that unusual for someone of Father Carey's sexual proclivities to meet a violent death, but not by poisoning; that method is so premeditated and I can't see any of his young partners, or perhaps I should say victims, doing that.'

'What about suicide?'

'Far too uncertain and unpleasant for one thing and for another, he wouldn't have been ignorant of the effects of death cap toadstools – there was a large textbook of medicine in his living room and I found a whole page on the subject. Don't look so downcast; murder enquiries are often like this to start with. Let's go along to the hospital, shall we? It's only a few hundred yards down the road and although I suspect it will be too late to catch any of the administrators, we might find Calvert in if we're lucky. I'd like to get on with something this evening as I'm tied up tomorrow and won't be free again until Thursday morning.'

The porter on duty at the reception desk in the front hall of St Cuthbert's Hospital was smartly dressed in a dark suit and his tie gave away the fact that he was ex-service, which Tyrrell would have guessed anyway from his neatly cut short hair and brisk, but polite manner as he dealt efficiently with a distraught-looking woman who was standing in front of them and then looked up alertly when she had walked away.

'How may I help you, sir?'

'I'd like to have a word with Mr Calvert, if it's at all possible,' he said showing the man his warrant card.

'You don't know the chaplain, do you, sir?'

'No, I don't.'

'Thought not. He likes to be called Father Calvert – very particular he is about it.'

'Is he married?'

The man raised his eyebrows almost imperceptibly. 'No, sir, he isn't. He lives in a self-contained basement flat under the nurses' hostel. I'll give him a call for you. Who shall I say it is? I'm afraid I didn't see your name on that card.'

'My name is Tyrrell, Chief Inspector Tyrrell. That won't mean anything to him, though, and perhaps you'd better tell him that it's about Father Carey.'

'Sad that, wasn't it? Lovely man. Always in here, he was. Full of life. Place won't be the same without him. Excuse me a moment.' He entered a number on the internal phone. 'Bleep Father Calvert for me, would you please, Fred? Gentleman and a lady to see him in the front hall. And tell him that it's about Father Carey.' He made a gesture towards some chairs in an alcove. 'If you'd like to take a seat over there, I don't suppose he'll be long. Like as not, he's on one of the wards.'

'What was Father Carey like?'

'Great big fellow – used to be a Rugby player. Liked a drink, too, and always had a cheerful word for us, not like.…'

As the porter looked over his shoulder, Tyrrell turned to see a man in a black suit and wearing a dog collar coming down the stairs towards them. He was small and neat, with horn-rimmed glasses, and although he must have been all of fifty his hair was thick and dark without a hint of grey in it.

'My name is Tyrrell, Chief Inspector Tyrrell, and this is my assistant, DC Sarah Prescott. I'm sorry to have descended on you like this – it's about Father Carey. We've just come from the presbytery and his housekeeper told us that you used to play chess with him.'

The man shook hands with them both without smiling. 'There's a room near the chapel where I see relatives of patients and I suggest we go there. Perhaps you'd follow me.'

The walk along the corridors was at least fifty yards and not once did the man say anything further or turn to look round at them.

'How may I help you?' he said, when they were all seated.

'The autopsy on Father Carey showed that he was poisoned and at this stage we're not sure whether it was murder or that he killed himself. I gather that you knew him well and we're interested to know what sort of person he was.'

Calvert put the tips of his fingers together. 'Patrick Carey was a very complicated man. He was a homosexual and, as you may imagine, that led to a great deal of guilt and he might just possibly have decided to end it all.'

'But would a Catholic priest commit suicide?'

'It's happened before.'

'You said he was a complicated person – in what way?'

'He was full of paradoxes. He liked to give the impression of being a hard-drinking, simple Irish peasant, but although the first part was undoubtedly true, he was neither simple, nor was he a peasant. He was completely wasted in that parish of his. In the nineteenth century, with all the Irish navvies working on the railways, both underground and overground, there was a flourishing Catholic community in this area, hence the large church and presbytery, but about ten years ago most of the people were moved to a new estate and those left behind were largely the elderly. As a result, Patrick didn't have enough to do and that's why he spent so much time here.'

'You said he was a homosexual – was he discreet about it?'

'I don't know. He told me about it one evening after our game of chess. I was going to say confessed, but it wasn't like that at all; he'd had a good deal to drink and it just came out. He wasn't in the mood for elaborating, or submitting to an inquisition for that matter, and so I didn't try to make him.'

'When was that?'

'About a year ago, if I remember correctly.'

'Did he ever mention it again?'

Calvert shook his head.

'And what about his chess skills?'

'How shall I put it? Strong on flair and attack, weak on analysis. I could almost never beat him if we played speed chess, but in the longer game, he'd often lose patience and do something stupid.'

'Did you play every week?'

'Without fail. The only exceptions were when one or the other of us was on holiday, or unwell, like the Thursday before he died. He spoke to me late that afternoon to tell me that he had a stomach upset and didn't feel up to it.'

'Did he seem very ill to you?'

'Not particularly, just a bit pale and not his usual cheerful self.'

'But not like someone who had recently poisoned themselves?'

'That's a very difficult question to answer. I've been called in to see any number of patients over the years who've attempted suicide and their reactions have been as diverse as their personalities. At one end of the scale, some are overcome with shame, guilt and depression, while others are almost euphoric and there has been every gradation in between. In any case, I only saw Patrick for a few moments on that occasion – we met in the front hall when he was about to give me a ring.'

'Well, thank you for being so helpful.'

'Any time. I shall miss Patrick. I was very fond of him and the place won't be the same without him.'

The chaplain showed them the way back to the front hall and when he had departed Tyrrell went across to the porter.

'I'd like to make an appointment to see the general manager, please.'

The man smiled. 'It's the chief executive now, sir, and, would you believe it, I'm no longer a porter, I'm the visitors' liaison officer. Anybody would think that giving us fancy names improves the shining hour, but, believe me it doesn't – if you ask me it's all a lot of bullshit, begging your pardon, miss. Anyway it's a Captain Boyd.'

'Captain?'

'Captain, RN,' the man said with heavy emphasis. 'He left the hospital about twenty minutes ago, but his secretary's probably still here – she often works late.'

They were in luck and after arranging to meet the chief executive at eight-thirty on the Thursday morning, they left the hospital and Tyrrell pointed to the pub across the road.

'I don't know about you, Sarah, but I've had enough for today. How about a drink?'

'What a good idea! Would you mind, though, if I made a phone call first?'

'Of course not. I won't be making you late for a date, will I?'

Sarah smiled ruefully. 'No such luck. It's just my father; he gets into a state if I don't arrive at exactly the time he's expecting me. He's quite old, you see, and rather set in his ways.'

That had been the understatement of the year, Sarah thought, after she had switched off her mobile. His reaction had been almost as extreme as if she had suddenly announced that she was going to Australia for a year. Why hadn't she warned him? It meant that he would have to miss a talk he wanted to hear on Radio Four. No, he never listened to the radio when he was eating; no, he couldn't possibly have supper any later than it would be anyway. As it was, he would be up half the night with indigestion and it was absurd to suggest that he might have something earlier – she knew perfectly well that he never ate between meals.

Even though Sarah was still seething when she joined Roger Tyrrell in the corner of the saloon bar, she fondly imagined that she had succeeded in hiding it from him, but, as before, he seemed to read her like a book.

'Problems?'

'Not really, just my father being cantankerous.'

For a moment Sarah thought that he was going to make some comment about it, but he merely nodded, asked her what she would like to drink and went up to the bar, coming back a few minutes later with two halves of lager.

'What did you think of Calvert?' he asked after he had taken a sip from his drink.

'Seemed pretty straightforward to me.'

'I agree. He looked rather severe and humourless on first acquaintance and the porter didn't seem to like him overmuch, but I rather took to him. Any feeling about him being gay?'

'Only the porter's obvious amusement when you asked if the man was married and it's true that he hardly gave me a glance, but that doesn't mean much.'

Tyrrell wasn't so sure; despite her straightforward manner and, he was quite convinced, sexual inexperience, there could be no denying the effect that Sarah had had on Tredgold and, for that matter, he had noticed the looks that several other men had given her as well.

'I expect we'll be able to get a better feel for him when we chat to a few people at the hospital on Thursday.'

'What do you hope to get out of the chief executive?'

Tyrrell reached into the breast pocket of his jacket, took out his wallet and passed the piece of paper, which he extracted from it, across to her.

'These are the notes that Father Carey made about a patient in the Intensive Therapy Unit; they are distinctly intriguing and I'm going to try to get permission to talk to him.'

'Locked in?' Sarah said, when she had finished reading it. 'I'm afraid it doesn't mean anything to me.'

'Neither did it to me at first, but then I remembered a book I read whilst at university, *Thérèse Raquin* by Emile Zola. Thérèse marries a rather anaemic young man called Camille Raquin and then she and her lover, Laurent, murder him. Unsuspected, they marry and Laurent joins Thérèse, who is already living with Camille's kindly mother. The two of them are tortured by guilt, their love turns to hate and after Madame Raquin suffers a stroke, which leaves her dumb and motionless with only the language of her eyes, Thérèse confesses to her what they have done. It is all too much for them, they commit suicide and Madame Raquin sits for a whole day with them at her feet, contemplating and feasting her eyes on them, brooding with hate. That's the gist of it.'

'I remember now. Wasn't there a TV production of it some years ago.'

'That's right and very powerfully done it was, too.'

'And this patient is in the same state as Madame Raquin?'

'It certainly sounds like it.' Tyrrell took another sip from his glass. 'How did you find today?'

'Better than I could have imagined. Of course I have been out in the field with Inspector Painter a few times, but only to take notes, and I haven't been allowed to do anything on my own.'

'I thought you coped with Mrs Flynn very well. This job has a great deal to do with handling people and getting their confidence; once you've done that, it's surprising how much they'll tell you.' He paused, put down his glass and looked straight at her. 'You do realize, though, that this job can play havoc with one's social life and domestic arrangements – and nine-to-five office hours, which is really what it's amounted to for you over the last nine months, are just not possible if you want to stay in the CID. Early starts, unexpected delays and occasional nights away are all part of it.'

'You're thinking about my father?'

'I did wonder how tied you are.'

'I'll be able to handle it.'

Tyrrell gave her a reassuring smile. 'I'm sure you will. Why not take tomorrow off and I'll look forward to seeing you on Thursday morning just before eight-thirty in the front hall of St Cuthbert's. All right?'

'I'll be there.'

Sarah rejected the detective's offer of a lift back to Fulham – she needed time to think. Even though she had only been working for Tyrrell for less than a day, she already liked him, was intrigued by the case and was excited by the prospect of following it through. What, though, was she going to do about her father? Predictably, he began to grumble as soon as she came through the door.

'It's too bad of you, Sarah. You know that I get indigestion if I eat late and that means that I won't be able to get to sleep.'

'I'm sorry, Father, but I was out on a case and I couldn't get to a phone any earlier.'

'I can't think why you ever went into the police force – it's no sort of job for a girl. I could easily have got you a post as a secretary in a legal firm as you seemed to be keen on the law; I didn't pay out a lot of money for that secretarial course for fun, you know.'

Sarah turned both to take the two packets out of the fridge and also to hide her expression of exasperation.

'It hasn't been wasted at all, Father, I use both my shorthand and typing regularly and I've told you any number of times how grateful I am for that course.'

He peered suspiciously at the two bowls, which she had just lifted down from a cupboard.

'What is it this time?'

'Cod steaks with parsley.'

'Not again!'

'We haven't had them for at least three weeks and you said then how much you'd enjoyed them then. Come on, Father, you know how much you like fish.'

'Why don't we ever have any fresh food? All this processed stuff's full of preservatives.'

'I cook fresh meals for you every weekend, as you well know.'

'You can keep that insolent tone out of your voice, Sarah.'

She put the wooden spoon down on the draining board with elaborate care.

'I was going to wait until after the meal to tell you, Father, but I may as well do so now. I've just been given the opportunity to work with one of the chief inspectors and from Thursday onwards it's going to mean irregular hours of work, even at weekends. Unless you'd prefer me to organize a cooked lunch through "meals on wheels" and leave your supper for you in the fridge, you'll have to learn how to use the microwave oven.'

In the stunned silence that followed, Sarah decided that she might as well press on – at least he hadn't said no straight away.

'Right, now is as good a time as any for the first lesson and, as I've got tomorrow off, we'll be able to go through it all again then. The most important thing to remember is never to put anything metallic into it, or switch it on when it's empty, but apart from that, it's simplicity itself. You empty the contents of the package you select into one of these bowls, cover it with a sheet of clingfilm from the roll here, make sure that you perforate it, set the timer for three minutes and press the start button. When the pinger goes, release the door catch, take the bowl out with a cloth, as it will get quite hot, remove the film and it's ready to eat. Now, watch how I do it with the first one and then you can have a try with the second.'

He half raised his hand and for one moment she had the scarcely credible thought that he was going to hit her, but she forced herself to look straight at him, neither flinching nor backing away.

'Father, you're not paying attention. Let's go over it again.'

Although she could see that he was literally shaking with rage, she was determined not to give way, staring him out until his shoulders drooped, he lowered his eyes and with sudden meekness began to follow her instructions. It was too good to last, she thought, and she was right; he only picked at his food and refused to talk to her for the rest of the evening. He continued in the same vein the next day, but she decided to carry on as if she had his full co-operation, stocking up the freezer, cleaning the flat and doing the outstanding washing and ironing.

How things had changed, she thought, as she got out of bed the following morning. Only two short days ago, she had overslept and could hardly bear the thought of going into work and now she was looking forward to getting back to the enquiry and escaping from her father, who was still sulking when she took in his morning cup of tea and again refused to speak to her.

CHAPTER FOUR

Captain Boyd was a pencil-slim, tall man with a rim of neatly cut hair around his deeply tanned scalp. His pale-blue eyes were sharp and intelligent and he got smartly to his feet as the two detectives were shown into his office.

'What can I do for you?' he asked when the introductions were over.

'It's about Father Carey. We are satisfied that he died from the effects of a poison and as I understand that he spent a great deal of time here, it seems a natural place at which to start our enquiries.'

'You said poisoned. How did that come about?'

'That's what we're here to find out, but I think it's safe to say that we have already ruled out the possibility of it being an accident. Did you know him at all yourself?'

'Knew what he looked like, of course, and passed the time of day with him on a couple of occasions, but that's all. You'd best try Calvert – he's our resident chaplain and what you might term an Anglo-Catholic himself.'

Tyrrell decided not to admit that he had already met the man and contented himself with nodding.

'The person I'd really like to talk to is one of your patients – a young man in the intensive therapy unit. I believe that Father Carey spent a great deal of time with him. Would you anticipate any difficulty with that?'

'It depends on what's wrong with him. Clifford Longley, the physician in charge of the unit, is a rather difficult man ... I tell you what, I'll see if I can raise Doctor Melrose on the phone and we'll see what she's got to say.'

'Doctor Melrose?'

'She's an anaesthetist and in my view one of the best people here. She's an expert on assisted respiration and, to be thoroughly indiscreet, from what I've heard she does most of the work on that unit.'

Boyd picked up the phone and dialled a number. 'Doctor Melrose? Alan Boyd here. The police have come to make some enquiries into Father Carey's death and the chief inspector would like a word with one of your patients.' He took the instrument away from his ear and covered it with his hand. 'What's the fellow's name?'

'Michael. That's all I know.'

'Michael,' he said into the receiver and then listened in silence for a minute or two. 'Right, I'll bring them up straight away.' The chief executive got to his feet. 'She's expecting Longley at about nine, so I said we'd meet her on the ward.'

Margaret Melrose was a slight young woman, who Tyrrell thought, couldn't have been much over the age of thirty-five. She was wearing a white blouse and navy-blue skirt under her white coat and her curly, dark hair was cut very short. She gave an initial impression of being serious and rather severe, but from time to time gave a smile, which completely transformed her face.

'Yes, Michael Donovan's the man you're after,' she said, after the detective had explained how he had found some notes about him on the priest's desk in the presbytery, 'and it's quite true that Father Carey spent a great deal of time with him.'

'Do you think I might have a word with him?'

'I don't see why not. In fact, I think it would be good for him, but I'll have to check with my colleague Doctor Longley first – he's officially in charge of his case. I'm afraid, though, that it won't be very rewarding.'

'Why not?'

'I don't know how Father Carey managed to keep up his visits; you see no one has been able to get a response out of Michael other than a yes and no achieved by one or two blinks. He is suffering from what is called "akinetic mutism".'

'The "locked in" syndrome?'

Tyrrell saw her look of surprise and respect and decided not to enlighten her about the priest's medical textbook.

'That's right. There are a number of causes and in Michael's case he had a congenital abnormality of the main artery at the base of his brain and following a blow to the head while playing Rugby, it must suddenly have expanded, starving the brainstem of blood and leaving him in the state he is in now. The poor man's brain is quite undamaged and he can both feel and understand everything, but he's only able to move his eyelids. As I said, that's the only way we can communicate with him – he gives one blink for yes and two for no.'

'How perfectly frightful! What did he do before the accident?'

'He was a solicitor, luckily unmarried and with no close family.'

'Isn't he even able to breathe on his own?' The woman shook her head. 'That's terrible. What are his chances of recovery or even some improvement?'

'Negligible, I'm afraid. He's already been here for nearly six months and there's been absolutely no change in his condition.'

'You mean he might stay in this state indefinitely?'

'That is a possibility, yes, but there's always the chance of the artery rupturing and— Ah, there's Doctor Longley.'

Through the window of the office, Tyrrell saw a stocky man wearing a white coat talking to the ward sister and a tall, pale young man, who had a stethoscope around his neck. The physician had thick brown hair and a neat moustache and although there was no hint of grey in either, his face was deeply lined and the detective thought that he was probably in his late fifties.

'I think it would be best if I have a word with him first; he needs to be handled with some care, does Doctor Longley, and if you don't have the knack....'

Doctor Melrose gave them a rather mirthless smile and left the room. Through the glass, Tyrrell saw the two of them in earnest conversation for a minute or two, then all four of them walked across to the bed in the far corner of the ward, returning almost at once. The physician gave the detective the most perfunctory of handshakes and Sarah a nod when he came into the office.

'I personally don't think this is a good idea at all, but Doctor Melrose disagrees and Michael seems to want to see you, although I can't think why. You're not to tire him out.'

'I understand that Father Carey used to spend at least an hour with him at a time.'

'Yes, he did, but he was sitting quietly here for most of the time giving him spiritual comfort.'

'I'm not exactly going to submit him to an inquisition, you know.'

Longley's upper lip twitched. 'I have at least the comfort of knowing that you wouldn't be able to achieve that even if you wanted to.'

'Did you know Father Carey well yourself?'

'No, I didn't. Religion, particularly of the sort that he practised, is not one of my interests. Now, if you'll forgive me, Doctor Pentland and I have another patient to see. Perhaps, Margaret, you would be good enough to join us as soon as you are free.'

Doctor Melrose didn't exactly say 'I told you so' as they left the office, but her wry expression made her meaning just as clear as if she had done so out loud.

'Michael,' she said, to the man lying motionless on the bed, 'this is Chief Inspector Tyrrell and his assistant, Miss Prescott; as I told you, they are enquiring into Father Carey's tragic death. Right, Chief Inspector, I'll be somewhere on the ward should you need me again.'

Michael Donovan's bed was one of four in the large open-plan ward. Each bay was fully equipped with piped gases, complicated monitors and breathing apparatus and, as Tyrrell glanced across the room, he saw that only one of the other beds was occupied and that by someone who was obviously unconscious. He sat down by the bedside and positioned himself so that he could see the man's eyes clearly.

'I'm afraid that I probably won't be much good at this to start with, but I hope you'll bear with me. I was particularly keen to meet you as I understand that Father Carey spent a lot of time talking to you and Doctor Longley told me that you wanted to see me. Is that right? The eyelids blinked once. Is it something to do with Father Carey that's worrying you?'

The affirmative blink was repeated. The man's face was

completely devoid of expression, but as the detective looked at him, wondering how to continue the interview, the eyelids began to move again. At first, Tyrrell didn't realize that there was a pattern to it, but then the penny dropped: there had been three short blinks, three long and then three short again.

'SOS?' he asked. 'Is that what you're signalling?'

'Yes,' the solitary blink conveyed.

'Are you afraid that we might be overheard?'

'Yes.'

'Don't worry, there's only one nurse in here and I'll make quite sure that she's out of earshot when I speak. Do you know the Morse code?'

'No.'

'Only SOS?'

'Yes.'

'Would you like to learn it?'

'Yes.'

'Right. I'll record it on to a cassette for you and come again when you're confident with it.'

'No.'

'Don't you want anyone else to know about it?'

'No.'

'In that case, we'll have the first lesson right away. A useful mnemonic for the dots when they occur on their own is "elephants in straw hats" for the dots – "e" is one dot, "i" two, "s" three and "h" four – and "two miles off" works the same way for the dashes. Have you got that?'

'Yes.'

'What is "m"?'

Two long blinks followed almost immediately and Tyrrell gave the lifeless, wasted hand on the sheet a gentle squeeze.

'Well done. Now, let's try a short sentence. "Is he Tom?" '

The sequence of short and long blinks came back accurately and quickly.

'Good man. I can see that you're going to be a champion at this. Now look, I learned Morse a long time ago when I was a small boy and I've forgotten some of it; I'll let you have the letters I'm confident with now, you'll be able to practise them and then I'll come back this evening with the remainder. All right?'

'Yes.'

'Is there anything else you'd like to know in the meantime?' he asked, after they had spent the next twenty minutes working on the code.

'Yes.'

It took the detective a good five minutes and many questions before he discovered that Donovan wanted to know how Father Carey had died.

'Death cap toadstool poisoning,' Tyrrell said, when he had finally understood. 'We don't yet know how he came to take them, but as he hated mushrooms, it doesn't seem likely that it happened accidentally and we still haven't decided whether he was poisoned or took them deliberately himself. No? You don't think he would have committed suicide? I see, that's very interesting; you must tell me why you're so sure later on. All right? Well, goodbye, Michael. I hope you don't mind if we use your first name; mine's Roger and this is Sarah. I'll be back at about seven.'

Tyrrell could see that Sarah was practically in tears as they left the intensive therapy unit and he didn't blame her, he felt much the same himself. The very thought of being in Donovan's position, even for half an hour, brought him out in a cold sweat and already the man had had to endure it for six months and with no end in sight.

'Let's go back to the office shall we? I've got some administrative ends to tie up and I'll also have to see what I can do about organizing a crash course in Morse for you. It's obvious that Michael's on to something and the sooner both of us are able to communicate with him the better. I'll try to put in as much practice as I can and I suggest that we both go to see him again tomorrow morning.'

'Is Morse still in use?'

'No, it was formally discontinued about a year ago. You're wondering if there are still any instructors about?'

'Yes.'

'I don't think you need worry about that. I know a retired army signals officer who helps us from time to time with codes and advice about bugging devices and if he doesn't know about Morse, no one will. He's been in communications since the middle of the war and worked at the centre at Cheltenham for a number of years. To be honest, he's as mad as a hatter; he's got an absolute obsession with the subject and sits up half the night picking up obscure broadcasts on his short-wave receiver.'

Sarah hadn't the least idea what to expect as she walked up the pleasant tree-lined road in Beckenham, but the small detached house looked to her to be conventional enough until she was half-way up the path and saw the forest of aerials attached to the chimney.

'Hello.'

Keyed up as she was, Sarah practically jumped out of her skin and whirled round to see the owner of the deep, booming voice getting to her feet.

'I'm sorry, I didn't see you.'

'You must be Sarah Prescott – I'm Madge Fordyce.'

Sarah's hand was taken in a grip that wouldn't have disgraced a navvy.

'Excuse the gardening kit, doing a spot of weeding. Harry's playing with one of his bits of electronic gadgetry – as usual. Follow me.'

Despite the parade-ground manner and her four-square figure, for which the battered, green pullover, tweed skirt and Wellington boots did nothing at all, there was a distinct twinkle in the woman's very blue eyes, which shone out of her deeply lined and tanned face.

'Open the door, would you? Don't want to get earth off me wellies on to the clean tiles.'

Sarah did so and then jumped again as the powerful voice went off like a foghorn over her shoulder.

'Harry! Sarah's here.'

On the train, Sarah had passed the time by trying to guess what Colonel Fordyce would look like, but none of her speculations was anywhere near the mark. He was a slightly built, scholarly-looking man, who was both softly spoken and polite. It was difficult to judge his age – he had kept his thick, sandy-coloured hair – and even though everything he did was carried out in a measured and careful fashion, he looked nothing like as old as she realized he must have been to have served during the war.

'And how's Roger Tyrrell? I haven't seen him for some time.'

'He's very well, thank you. He sent his best wishes.'

'Thank you. Please return them. I often think the word nice is overworked, but it describes him perfectly, wouldn't you agree?'

'Yes, I certainly would. I've only just started working for him, but the contrast between him and my last boss is striking to say the least of it.'

The man smiled, nodding at the same time, then put the tips of his fingers together. 'Now, what's the problem?'

Sarah told him in a few short sentences and when she had finished, the man nodded.

'So the patient is able to understand your spoken speech without any difficulty, but you need to be able to decipher the Morse signals he is making by means of blinks?'

'Yes, that's exactly it.'

The man smiled. 'And how much time have we got?'

'The rest of today.'

'Well, in that case we'd better get started, hadn't we?'

Although Colonel Fordyce was infinitely patient, he was also a hard taskmaster and after three hours, Sarah's head was aching with the effort and she had almost been driven to screaming point by the incessant beeping of the transmitter.

'Had enough?' he asked, when he saw her massaging the back of her neck.

She was hardly even tempted to take a break, let alone give up, the sight of the prostrate figure in the ITU of St Cuthbert's Hospital in her mind's eye being enough to steel her to further effort.

'No, but do you think we could move on to eye blinks now?'

The man smiled and shook his head. 'Not just yet, but let's have a cup of tea, otherwise I'll never hear the last of it. I've no doubt that Madge will have had the kettle on the boil for a good half-hour already. She suffers from the delusion that I'm in a permanent state of dehydration, not to mention malnutrition.'

He left the room and returned a few minutes later accompanied by his wife and carrying a tray laden with a massive fruit cake and a plate of home-made shortbread.

'You look worn out, my dear,' Mrs Fordyce said, 'what has this terrible man been doing to you?'

'You've no need to worry about her, Madge, my dear, she's as tough as old boots – I was the one who had to beg for a break.'

'That'll be the day. Don't let him bully you, my dear.'

To her surprise, Sarah found the blinks much easier to follow than the aural version and was also able to appreciate the reasons for Fordyce's insistence on her getting a thorough grounding by ear first. He wasn't able to transmit anything like so rapidly using his eyes and the boost to her morale when she found herself understanding him quite easily was enormous.

'I think it's time for a real conversation,' he said, after a further hour had gone by. 'I'm sure you're ready for it and that is the object of the exercise, is it not?' Sarah nodded. 'Right, from now on I'll confine myself to blinks and you can use plain language back, just as you'll be doing with the patient. All set?'

Sarah moved her chair a fraction and watched anxiously as he began.

'What family do you have?'

'Just my father. We live together in a flat overlooking the river in Fulham – it's quite near the football ground.'

Sarah had a sudden panic as she glanced up at the clock on the mantelpiece and saw that it was already ten past six and that there would be no possibility of getting back home in time to get her father's supper.

'I'm so sorry, but I hadn't taken in how the time had slipped by. Would you think it the most awful cheek if I asked to use your phone? You see, my father is quite old and I ought to warn him that I'm going to be late.'

'Go ahead,' the colonel signalled. 'It's over there. I'll leave you in peace for a moment or two.'

Sarah was hardly aware that she had picked up the

message without any difficulty at all, being far too worried about how her father was going to react. In the event, he was every bit as tetchy as she had expected, but at least he condescended to speak to her.

'I know I'll get it wrong,' he said in his most querulous voice. 'The wretched thing's bound to give me an electric shock. Why couldn't you have given me proper notice that you were going to change the nature of your job and then I would have had time to get used to it.'

'I've already explained, Father, I only heard about it three days ago. You'll be all right – I've written down all the instructions for you on the pad beside the oven and I'm sure it will go smoothly. You can tell me about it when I get back – I won't be late.'

The telephone gave a brief ting as she replaced the receiver and Colonel Fordyce came back into the room almost immediately.

'Is your father all right?' he signalled.

'As all right as he'll ever be if I'm not there to do everything for him.'

'That obviously came from the heart.'

'I didn't mean it to sound like that. He is, after all, seventy-six and I can't expect him to change overnight. My mother had been ill for several years before she died ten years ago, my father had already retired and I took over the housekeeping from her. I suppose I ought to have made sure right from the start that he learned to cook, did the shopping and some of the housework, but you don't think of that sort of thing when you're fourteen. If it hadn't been for my uncle, my mother's brother, I doubt if I would ever have done a proper job, but he encouraged me when I decided to go into the police force. At first, when I was doing nothing more than office hours, it was easy enough to cope, but now that I'm at last out in the field, it's going to be quite another matter. Still, I love it and I'm quite determined to make a go of it.'

'I don't have any doubt about that. Now, you won't get swollen-headed, will you, if I tell you that you've picked up Morse as quickly as anyone I can remember? Most people are able to send competently after a few hours, but receiving's always more difficult. I realize that I'm not much good at this blinking business, but you're actually waiting for me. I can see it.' Fordyce gave a stretch and then began to use his voice. 'I don't know about you, but I've had enough for today. In any case, all you need now is practice and you can easily get that with your patient. You must be hungry after all your hard work; Madge and I would be so pleased if you'd stay for supper, but we'd quite understand if you feel you ought to go.'

Sarah hardly hesitated. 'I'd love to, if it's not too much of an imposition.'

'It would be the very reverse. We, or it would be fairer to say I, don't entertain nearly enough. Madge has her cronies she meets at the allotments and her work for the blind and she's always going on at me for being such a stick-in-the-mud. Still, as I've told her often enough, she ought to be getting used to me after fifty-four years of marriage.'

It didn't require the exercise of much mental arithmetic for Sarah to realize that both the Fordyces must be several years older than her father and yet they might have been a good ten years younger. Her father had become fossilized, tetchy and completely lacked interest in the present, whereas both of them were alert and quick both mentally and physically.

Sarah thoroughly enjoyed that evening. There was a

delicious casserole, baked apples with raisins and cream and finally coffee and mouth-watering chocolates. Apart from that, they both kept her entertained with stories of their travels and some of the extraordinary people they had met.

'All that makes my life seem very dull,' she said, after Fordyce had finished recounting a tale of a landing he had made into occupied France during the war. 'I've never even been abroad.'

'Well, you must certainly do so before you're very much older. Wouldn't it be possible for you to get someone to look after your father for a couple of weeks?'

'My Uncle Henry has offered to have him to stay often enough, but the two of them don't get on and Father's always refused to go.'

Not getting on was hardly the right expression, Sarah thought, as she sat on the train on the way back to London; relations between the two men could hardly have been worse. It had all started when she was sixteen and the cause had been something quite trivial. She had forgotten to collect the book that her father had ordered at the library on her way back from school; he had spoken to her sharply and she had answered back. In truth, it had been a half-hearted blow, but his signet ring had caught her lip and cut it quite badly. Henry Garnett was furious when he saw her the next day, gently touched her lip, which had had to have a stitch in it and had swollen up in spectacular fashion.

'You can tell that desiccated old tyrant that if he so much as touches you again, I'll— No, that wouldn't be fair; I'll do the deed myself, right now.'

Despite her entreaties, he had been as good as his word, driving round to the flat with her and telling her to wait in the car until he returned. She never did discover what passed between the two men, but her uncle came back looking distinctly pleased with himself and her father was noticeably subdued for many days after. As far as she knew, they hadn't spoken to one another since, all communications being through her.

'Tell your uncle that I have no wish to stay at his place in Sussex, even if he is not there himself,' he had said when her uncle invited her to go on holiday to France with him.

Sarah would have given anything to go – what could have been more exciting than a visit to Paris, even if her uncle would be working most of the time – but her father had developed sciatica two days before she was due to leave, making the most tremendous fuss and that was that. Why, oh why, had she been so weak? It was true that she had been only seventeen at the time and her father had been insidiously exerting more and more control over her for several years, but she wasn't seventeen any longer and those days were over, for good.

Her father was reading in bed when she got back and when he refused to talk to her, muttering something under his breath when she said goodnight, it was only too obvious that the battle had been well and truly joined and her future was going to depend on the result.

CHAPTER FIVE

After the detectives had gone, Michael Donovan closed his eyes, oblivious to the sound of the respirator and even the presence of the medical team that was clustered around the bed of the unconscious woman in the far corner of the ward. Ten minutes later, he still hadn't got over the fact that for the first time since his accident he had had the chance to communicate with someone properly. Why was it that Tyrrell had picked up the SOS at once and immediately realized the implications of it, whereas he had tried it several times both with Doctor Melrose and Doctor Pentland and they had failed to recognize it? The short answer, he reckoned, was that neither of them wanted to communicate with him; it would have meant providing answers to awkward questions that would have proved altogether too painful for them.

Donovan had had very little contact with the police in his life and his mental image of them had been either of avuncular Mr Plods, or else of aggressive, ruthless men, who enjoyed putting the boot in. The fact that the police wanted to talk to him at all was the first surprise – how had they known about his special relationship with Father Carey – and the second had been the chief inspector and his assistant. Not only had Tyrrell proved to be remarkably quick on the uptake, but like Father Carey the man seemed to have known intuitively what he was thinking. Apart from that, he had spoken to him immediately as a person, not as an object, and as to the young WPC, she hadn't said anything to him, but her smile had been natural and unembarrassed and he liked young women who didn't conform to the currently fashionable pale and anorexic image. She had a fresh complexion, no need of make-up and her figure could best be described as cuddly. As soon as he had had the thought, though, and the mental image of it, he found it so upsetting that he deliberately turned his mind to other things. There was not only the Morse Code to occupy him, but also Father Carey's death. Surely the man must have been murdered – why else would an officer as senior as a chief inspector have been sent to the hospital – and if that were the case, was there a clue in all those confidences that the priest had let out in his long monologues?

True to his word, Tyrrell did return that evening and spent forty-five minutes with him, going over the letters he had already learned and the remainder that the detective hadn't been able to remember.

'Steady on,' Tyrrell said, when they were having a last run through, 'you're getting far too quick for me. I've sent young Sarah on a crash course in Morse and I'll have to have some practice sessions with her, otherwise I can see that I'm never going to be able to keep up with you.'

'Any more news?' Donovan signalled.

'Only that we discovered that the poison was in the whiskey in Carey's silver flask, which we found in the hip pocket of his black suit. Evidently alcohol doesn't neutralize the toxin produced by the death cap toadstool.'

'So he must have been murdered? The poison could hardly have been there by accident and I can't see him having committed suicide like that.'

'It certainly looks like it.'

'How long does the poison take to act?'

'The first symptoms appear from six to twelve hours after ingestion, so I'm told.'

'That would fit.'

'Fit with what.'

'Father Carey arranged for me to attend Mass and he was taken ill the same evening. Just before the Mass, he made a joke about the hip flask and left it on the table behind my bed; someone must have added the poison while he was at the altar.'

'Tell me about it in detail tomorrow when I come back here. You must be tired and they'll be shooing me out at any moment. Incidentally, no one here knows about the nature of the poison used and I don't want the information to get out.'

'I won't say a word to anyone about it, even if I could. On your side, you will keep quiet about the Morse, won't you?'

'You think that someone murdered him, then?'

'I'm quite sure of it.'

'Don't worry, it'll be a secret between the two of us and Sarah.'

'Give her my love.'

'I will. Goodnight, Michael.'

'Goodnight, Roger, and thank you.'

Roger Tyrrell gave him a bright smile as he squeezed his hand, but he felt more like crying. It wasn't only the fact that the man's intelligence was so clearly unaffected, but that he still had an interest in an attractive girl. He was so preoccupied as he left the unit that he almost cannoned into the figure who came out of one of the doors on the landing above the front hall.

'I'm so sorry, I wasn't looking where I was going.'

'That's all right. You're from the police, aren't you?'

'That is correct. Chief Inspector Tyrrell.'

'I'm the night sister, Claire Garrard. How did you find Michael?'

'To be honest, I don't know how to answer that question; someone in his condition is right outside my experience.'

In fact, Tyrrell found the pale woman in uniform far more difficult to talk to than Donovan. Her voice was so soft as to be practically inaudible and she kept her eyes fixed firmly no higher than the middle button of his jacket, never once looking up at his face. She also seemed anxious to keep the conversation going and yet, at the same time, seemed to be scared stiff of him.

'How did you manage to communicate with him so well?'

It had taken her a long time to get it out and the detective's interest quickened when he realized that it was the question she had been wanting to ask him all along.

'How do you mean?'

'You must have been with him for nearly an hour.'

'If you mean talking, I hardly did any, but there's a great deal more to communication than that. I asked him if he would like me to sit with him for a time and he signalled that he would. I think he has been terribly upset by Father Carey's death; from what I gathered from the medical staff this morning, Michael had had hardly any visitors at all apart from him, so it's hardly surprising that he welcomed some non-medical company. What sort of person was Father Carey?'

'He used to drink too much and it's difficult to have respect for a man who does that, particularly when he's a priest.'

Although the night sister hadn't looked up, Tyrrell could see that she was as tense as a coiled spring; the fingers of her right hand were playing nervously with the material of her dress and there was a pulse beating rapidly in her neck.

'Fordyce was most impressed by you, Sarah,' Tyrrell said the following morning. 'He took the trouble to ring me up last night and told me how well you'd got on with the Morse. Well done. That's a great deal more than I can say for my experience at the hospital last night; when I went to see Michael I found it the most terrible struggle.'

'Did he have a problem with it then?'

'No, it was me. He already signals away like a machine gun. You're obviously going to be a great deal quicker at it than me and what I suggest is that you write down his answers in shorthand and then read them back to me. Otherwise, I'm bound to lose the thread and hold the proceedings up. I've arranged for us to go there in about half an hour when Longley is safely caged in his out-patient clinic. It should be an interesting session; Michael got quite excited when I told him about the poison being in the whiskey in Carey's hip flask.'

'I didn't know about that.'

'Tredgold rang to tell me about it yesterday afternoon. It seems that the flask was left on a table behind Donovan's bed when he was taken down to the chapel for a special Mass and it sounds very much as if that was when the deed was done. That's why I'm particularly anxious to hear about the Mass in detail.' Tyrrell leaned back in his chair and looked at her across the desk. 'How are things at home?'

'Armed neutrality at the moment.'

'That's better than active hostilities, I suppose, but seriously, you will say if you need any time off to sort things out, won't you?'

'Everything's fine, thank you. I've got him to do some cooking now and he'll soon settle into it. If I know him, he'll soon be telling me that it was his own idea all along.'

What else had Fordyce been saying apart from praising her skill at Morse, Sarah wondered? Why had she said so much to the man? If once Tyrrell got it into his head that she was chained to her father, there would be no hope of her being able to continue to work for him, let alone of advancing her career in the CID.

When they arrived at the ITU, as Tyrrell had hoped, Longley was out of the way and Doctor Melrose was supervising the investigation of a patient with a severe muscle problem in the sleep study room and so they were able to spend the best part of an hour on their own with Donovan. Once Tyrrell had explained about Sarah taking down his signals in shorthand, they both sat down by the bed and he adjusted the mirror so that Michael was able to see their faces.

'I'm particularly interested in the Mass that Father Carey said for you on that Sunday. Was it his suggestion or yours?'

'His. You must remember that with him, all I could do was signal "yes" and "no", but for all that, he was remarkably adept at guessing what I was thinking.'

'Who was there?'

'For a start, practically everyone who had had anything to do with my care. I think Carey must have gone round drumming up support and then it probably became a matter of face for everyone to turn up. Patrick once told me that they were a Godless lot, with the exception of Doctor Pentland, who is a keen Catholic.'

'Could you give me some names?'

'Well, starting from the top, as it were, Doctor Longley was fussing about as usual, sticking his oar in, although I don't believe he knows how half the apparatus works – he just pretends he does. Doctor Melrose, Doctor Pentland, Doctor Lee, Jacquie and Liz, my regular physiotherapist and nurse, were keeping an eye on things and Sister Mountfield was sitting nearby.'

'Who is Doctor Lee?'

'The senior house officer. She's only just come to work here and she's hardly had anything to do with my care. There were quite a few others, but I didn't recognize anyone else's voice; you have to remember that my field of vision was very restricted as the mirror had been positioned so that I could see the altar. No, wait a moment, I was forgetting Sister Garrard.'

'The night sister?'

'Yes.'

'And you told me yesterday that Father Carey left his hip flask on the table behind your bed.'

'Yes. He made a joke about it, saying that some time back one of his superiors had noticed its outline in his hip pocket when he was saying Mass and he never heard the last of it. He asked me to keep an eye on it for him.'

'But you weren't able to see it?'

'No.'

'Could any of those people you mentioned have got to it during the Mass?'

'Yes, most of them quite easily.'

'Have you been able to form any impression of the people here? What about Father Carey as a start?'

'He was a marvellous man. He showed me more compassion and understanding of my condition than all the doctors and nurses put together. You can't imagine how important he was to me. As I have no close family at all and all my so-called friends disappeared from the scene after a week or two, he was the one person who kept me sane. And then there was his fight for AIDS victims. He didn't give me all the details, but I gathered that there had been a major row at the hospital over it, not least in this very unit. Longley and Sister Garrard appear to have objected to their presence on moral grounds, thinking that the sufferers had brought it on themselves and should be shut away in special isolation units, whereas there were those like Doctor Melrose, Sister Mountfield and Father Carey himself, who thought that such an attitude was an affront to humanity and the medical profession in particular. That was what his sermon was about and he really let them have it hot and strong. Carey also hinted to me that both Longley and Sister Garrard were hypocrites. He implied that the former was an adulterer and made a remark about Sister Garrard to the effect that it was all very well for her to go around taking moral stances when she was nothing like so pure as she made out. He even had a dig at Doctor Melrose for her feminist views.'

'Of all the people you've come across here or heard about, who do you consider the most trustworthy?'

The reply was almost instantaneous. 'Doctor Melrose and Sister Mountfield. Doctor Melrose may be a bit abrupt and she is aggressively feminist, but she's the one who does most of the work around here and, as for Sister

Mountfield, she's just a thoroughly nice woman, steady, reliable and unflappable.'

'Would either of them had access to the hip flask?'

'Not Sister Mountfield. She was sitting in my line of vision the whole time and I'm quite sure that she didn't move until the Mass was over and Father Carey had picked up his flask on his way back to the vestry.'

'Where is the vestry?'

'My bed was some two or three feet in front of the door; there wasn't much of a gap because I remember hearing Father Carey having to squeeze between the bed and the table to get to it.'

'What about Jacquie and Liz?'

'I think that for both of them, working here is just a job, like any other one, not that there's anything wrong with that – the same could have been applied to me. They like a gossip and, to be honest, used to annoy me by talking across me as if I wasn't there.'

'And finally we come to Doctor Pentland.'

'If you ask me, Doctor Pentland is a worried man – I'm quite certain that there's something on his mind. He always seems preoccupied and if I were Jacquie and Liz, I would watch out – I wouldn't be at all happy about the looks he gives them.'

Tyrrell didn't know about Donovan and Sarah, but at the end of the hour, even though they had been interrupted by visits from Jacquie, the physiotherapist, and one of the nurses who came to check the respirator, he was utterly drained by the effort of having concentrated for so long.

'We have to go now, Michael. We have a lot of information to work on and I'll keep you posted on our progress.'

'May I see you on your own for a moment?'

Sarah got up at once, closing her shorthand pad. 'I'll wait for you outside, sir. Goodbye, Michael.'

Tyrrell turned away from the bed several minutes later and was making his way towards the door when he saw Sarah signalling to him through the window of the sister's office.

'Sister Mountfield has very kindly offered us a cup of coffee in here,' she said, when she had made the introductions.

'How very nice of you, but won't we be in the way?'

'Not at all, sir. I'll be busy with one of the student nurses at the bedside for the next half an hour and you won't be disturbed in here.'

The detective drank his coffee slowly, not speaking and looking through the window into the ward.

'I don't know about you, Sarah, but I find this place unutterably depressing.'

'Me, too. I can't get the likelihood of what's going to happen to that poor young man out of my mind; as far as I can see he could go on living like that indefinitely.'

'I know. It doesn't bear thinking about. Let's go for a walk, shall we?'

It was a mellow, early autumn day and after twenty minutes they found a wooden seat in one of the surprisingly secluded small parks, that were liberally scattered around that part of London, and sat down on it.

'What do you make of it all, Sarah?'

She waited for a moment or two before replying, marshalling her thoughts.

'I don't think there can be any doubt that Father Carey was murdered. Not only does it seem that he was full of life just before he died, for one thing organizing that Mass for Michael, but I can't believe that he would have used a poison like that. He clearly didn't like mushrooms and even if he had decided to kill himself in that way, why didn't he just eat them, rather than extracting the juice and putting it into his whiskey?'

'He might have done it to disguise the taste.'

'That seems a bit far-fetched to me; he didn't leave a note and Michael seems convinced that he wasn't the type to commit suicide. If he was murdered, I suppose that one of his homosexual partners could have been responsible, but as you said, it is unlikely that teenagers would have done anything quite so calculated and killings under those circumstances are, I believe, usually impulsive and violent. I also think that Michael's suggestion that the poison was put into the flask during the Mass sounds like the most convincing explanation.'

Tyrrell nodded. 'I agree with you and if we're both correct, it makes it specially important to get a clearer picture of exactly what happened during the Mass. Sister Mountfield seems to be in the clear, but I'll still have a word with her about it, then I thought I'd see what I can make of Doctor Longley. The other three doctors will have to wait until next week.'

'What about me?'

'I'd like you to chat up Jacquie and Liz and also see what you can find out about Claire Garrard, the night sister. Now, she intrigues me. I met her briefly yesterday evening and I— No, I won't prejudice you about her, I'd like you to make your own mind up, but having said that, you won't let her know that we're particularly interested in her, will you? Incidentally, it was about her that Michael wanted a quiet word with me on my own – he thought what he had to say might embarrass you. Evidently she lifted up the sheet, which was his only covering, one night and had a good look. He thinks she might have done rather more than look if she hadn't been disturbed, and shall I say that he was convinced that her interest wasn't exactly professional. I suppose I'd better speak to Miss Beaumont, the chief nursing officer, as well; if she finds out that we've been questioning her charges behind her back, there'll be hell to pay if my past experiences of enquiries at hospitals are anything to go by. Let's go, shall we?'

It was clearly going to be easy enough to chat to Jacquie and Liz, Sarah thought, as she waited for Roger Tyrrell in the office outside Miss Beaumont's room, but she hadn't the first idea how even to begin to tackle night sister. Her train of thought was interrupted by the grey-haired woman, who gave a deep sigh as she rubbed out a name on the enormous whiteboard on the wall and wrote in another with a wax pencil.

'Sounds bad,' Sarah said.

The woman gave her a rueful smile. 'It is. Fixing the duty roster is rather like trying to do a jigsaw puzzle with a third of the pieces missing and another third from the wrong box. The big problem,' she said, as Sarah got up to stand beside her, 'is that nursing is no longer a job that most young women want to do, at least not in London. The pay's terrible, the hours irregular and there are much more attractive options by the score. Do you know, we're just over twenty-five per cent under establishment and we can't fill all the vacancies with temps? In the first place, the agencies can't cope with the demand and in the second, a lot of the girls they have to offer haven't had the training for the particular job required.'

'It must be a nightmare.'

'It is, particularly with the sickness rate being as high as it is at the moment. In my view, that's another indication of how little many of them care; in the old days, the merest sniffle wouldn't have meant a week off.'

'What's the night shift like?'

'One of the worst. I just don't know how we're going to manage this coming weekend, for example. If it hadn't been for Sister Garrard, we'd have been in much greater trouble over the last few weeks – she's always prepared to do extra duty – but I can't ask her again. If I were to do so, it would be just like her to cancel her arrangements without telling me and it was pure chance that I found out that she is due to go away for the day on Saturday. Not that she'd tell me about her plans, oh dear me no, but she came in here to borrow a railway timetable for the journey to Exeter and, do you know, she wasn't even aware of how good the coach service was, or how cheap? It's much easier, too, to get to Victoria from here than Paddington and, as I told her, if she caught the eight-thirty coach, she'd be in Exeter before lunchtime. She's so unworldly it isn't true and I do worry about her. She looks so pale and thin, but I have to admit that she's never off sick.'

'Long spells of night duty must make one's social life extremely difficult.'

'I don't know how they put up with it, but some people seem to like it.'

'Has Sister Garrard been doing it for long?'

'Ever since I've been here and that's eighteen months now. She even lives here – in one of the sisters' flats. I can understand someone wanting to be on the spot to start with when they're finding their feet, but not on a permanent basis.'

'Do you find it difficult to get people to nurse in the ITU?'

'We've been lucky in having the same sister for a number of years, but most of the nurses don't stay for very long – too much of a strain I suppose. You should see some of the girls the agencies send us – they don't know one end of a respirator from another. Oh, curse it!' She went across to the telephone and lifted the receiver. 'Nursing office.' The woman raised her eyebrows at Sarah as she listened. 'How long is she going to be off? ... A week? Just for a sore throat? ... But they all say it's suspected glandular fever ... Yes, I know it's not your fault, thanks for letting me know. Goodbye.'

The woman thumped the receiver back down on its cradle just as Tyrrell came out of the adjoining room with a tall, severe-looking woman in a grey jumper and matching skirt.

'Thank you, Miss Beaumont. As I said, we'll aim to interrupt the routine of your staff as little as possible. May I introduce my assistant DC Sarah Prescott?'

The woman inclined her head and stood there unblinking as they walked out.

'I doubt if I could take more than ten minutes of her,' Tyrrell said, with a rueful smile as they descended the staircase to the front hall. 'How about a bite of lunch? I spotted a reasonable looking pub up the road as we came in.'

Sarah didn't feel like tackling Jacquie after lunch and Liz was off duty; there would be time to see them later and that left the weekend for trying to find out as much as she could about Claire Garrard. But how was she going to make a start? She had already seen on the wall chart in the nursing office that the night sister had the next three nights off and if she was going to spend the weekend away in Exeter, it would hardly be practical to interview her, particularly as Roger Tyrrell had been most insistent that the woman shouldn't realize that they were interested in her. It wasn't even as if there was anyone in the hospital with whom she might be able to discuss the problem, let alone from whom she might pick up some gossip. She needed someone who was both completely trustworthy and who could not possibly have had anything to do with Father Carey's death. When she came to think about it, the answer had been staring her in the face all along; it had to be Michael Donovan and she decided to visit him again that evening.

'And so you see,' she said, after she had explained the situation to him, 'I'm desperately keen to make a success of this so that I won't have to go back to work with that dreadful man Inspector Painter.'

'Why don't you follow the woman to Exeter?'

It was the first time that Sarah had tried the Morse with Michael on her own and it went extremely smoothly, much more so than it had done with Fordyce.

'I always could, I suppose, but I doubt if it would be very rewarding.'

'You never know. You may come up with something surprising. You forget that I was once a solicitor specializing in divorce cases and the most unlikely people get up to some very strange antics. There's something distinctly odd about Sister Garrard. I've heard the other nurses gossiping about her; only the other day one of them was saying that she never goes away, spending all her time either on duty or in her flat. Why, in that case, the sudden visit to Exeter? And there's another thing. I told you about Father Carey's sermon, didn't I?'

'Some of it.'

'Well, there's someone dying of AIDS in the isolation

room attached to this unit and some of the doctors and nurses, including Sister Garrard take a less than charitable view of his presence. They don't think that St Cuthbert's should take AIDS patients at all and I gather that there has been talk of a petition to the chief executive. Anyway, Carey had a real go at those who take that view and pretty compelling stuff it was, too.'

'What does Sister Garrard look like?'

'I'm not very good at this, I'm afraid, typical male! In my defence, though, I've only ever seen her in uniform. She's quite tall, I'd say about five foot eight, she's very pale with fair hair and rather striking eyes and she must be in her late twenties. She has regular features and doesn't wear any make-up. In fact, she'd be quite pretty if only she had a spark of animation in her. She walks about like a cross between Florence Nightingale and a zombie. No, now I come to think about it, that's not true, she has a distinct limp – her hip drops down on one side, I think the right.'

'You've done exceptionally well. What hairstyle does she have?'

'You'll laugh at me when I tell you that I haven't noticed, but in my defence I've only ever seen her with her cap on and that hides most of it. It is cut short, though. It would never have done for a solicitor to dirty his hands with any detective work, but I've always had a childish ambition to follow someone; I imagine that it's a lot more difficult than it sounds.'

'I can see that you're quite determined that I should go after her.'

'I am. Tell me how you'd set about it.'

Sarah didn't like to admit that she'd never followed anyone other than in a training exercise and tried to put on a show of confidence that she certainly didn't feel.

'Well, let's see, now. The one good thing is that she's never seen me before and I'd try to make myself as inconspicuous as possible by wearing neutral clothes such as a blouse and skirt and I could introduce a bit of variety by taking my two-coloured reversible raincoat and hat.'

'What would you do if she got into a taxi and there wasn't another one waiting?'

'That's where we have an unfair advantage; I'd ring the Exeter police and ask them to meet the bus or train with an unmarked car. Unless Claire Garrard has something to hide or else is seriously paranoid, she's unlikely to suspect that she's being followed and that should make it a lot easier. If we were following someone like a suspected terrorist, we would have relays of people on the job.'

'Sounds rather fun.'

Sarah laughed. 'To be honest, I was having you on just now; I've never followed anyone in earnest, not even in training, I've merely been instructed in the technique, but those who have tell me that it's as boring as hell and I bet you that she'll just be visiting a great aunt, who's been taken ill and needs to be settled into an old people's home.'

'What do you bet me?'

It was as if someone had dropped an ice cube down the back of her shirt. Michael's face may have been devoid of any expression and yet she knew which way his thoughts were moving as surely as if he had given her a nudge and a wink. What made it ten times worse was that his remark had provoked a physical sensation so localized and intense that she blushed scarlet. Keep it light, she said to herself, please God let me handle it the right way.

'You're nothing but a dirty old man, Michael Donovan, and you a solicitor.'

She leaned forward and gave him a kiss on the cheek.

'You will follow her, won't you?'

'I'll think about it.'

Sarah stood for a moment in the corridor outside the ITU, her heart hammering inside her chest and cursing herself for letting things get out of control. How many times in her training course had she been told never to get emotionally involved with anyone during an enquiry? And yet here she was having held Michael's hand while she talked to him, no doubt by subtle pressure of her fingers and the inflexion of her voice giving him the impression that their relationship was more than a professional one. Was it merely an impression? She knew perfectly well that it wasn't; Michael had obviously been a most attractive man and even without the ability to speak a word or move anything other than his eyelids, his courage and intelligence still shone through. What sort of bet had he had in mind? Sarah had ideas about that, which is what had made her blush in the first place, and to get her mind off it, she ran down the stairs and then, seeing the lights on in the chapel, paused for a moment outside, then pushed the door open and went in.

CHAPTER SIX

Richard Pentland went into the chapel, sat down at the end of the pew halfway up the aisle and buried his face in his hands. He was off duty for the weekend, but couldn't face his parents and yet the thought of hanging around the hospital was even worse. He raised his head and, as he looked at the stained-glass window, he felt the tears start to roll down his cheeks and pulled his handkerchief out of his pocket. He made no attempt to control himself, remaining hunched up until the flood of emotion had passed and then sat back, drying his eyes and feeling calmer than he had for days. He let out a deep sigh and was just about to drop forward on to his knees, when the door behind him gave a loud creak and he whirled round, half rising to his feet.

'I'm sorry, I didn't mean to disturb you.'

'That's all right. I was just about to leave anyway.'

He got to within a few feet of the young woman standing by the door before he realized who it was and felt the cold shiver go right through him.

'I was just going to have a few quiet minutes in here at the end of a very long day,' she said, giving him a smile, 'but not meaning to be irreverent, I'm not sure that a drink wouldn't do me more good. Do you know of a decent pub around here?'

Richard Pentland was tired, he was desperately lonely and what possible harm could come, he thought, from having a drink with the pleasantly plump and fresh-complexioned young woman. She seemed friendly enough and although he knew precious little about the CID and even less about women police officers, it seemed to him unlikely that she would be all that bright. If he played his cards correctly, he might even discover the way the chief inspector was thinking, but on the other it wouldn't do to be seen by any of the others at the hospital.

'The pubs around here are a bit rough, but I do know one on the south side of the river where they do excellent meals. There's even a terrace overlooking the water, although it's a bit cold for sitting outside at this time of the year. I'm off duty this evening and I'd be glad to take you in my car if you'd like the company, but do say if you'd rather be on your own.'

He wasn't able to see her face in the poor light, but there was no hesitation in her voice.

'That would be very nice indeed; I wasn't relishing the idea of having to go back home and do some cooking.'

Pentland was tongue-tied at the best of times and even more so in the company of women, but a large gin, swiftly followed by another, made him for once feel at ease as well as warm and relaxed.

'It must be very exhausting working on the ITU for any length of time.'

'You can say that again. I'm nearly at the end of my six-month stint, thank God!'

'So Michael was already there when you arrived.'

'No, but he was one of the very first patients I had to look after and I'm ashamed to have to admit that I ran out of things to say to him after a fortnight. If you ask me, it was a thousand pities that he survived; he could easily last another year or more in the state he's in now.'

'I imagine it must be particularly difficult working with such a small team; don't you get on each other's nerves at times?'

'It's been one long nightmare, if you must know. Longley can't keep his hands off anything in a skirt, which means he always likes to have a female SHO; how I hate working with female SHOs, especially the one we have at the moment.'

'What's an SHO?'

Pentland looked up at the young policewoman, hardly able to believe his ears; what on earth were they doing sending someone to a hospital on an enquiry who didn't even know that?

'A senior house officer – that's the post immediately junior to the one I've reached. Most of them have never done any intensive care work and I have to supervise and teach them.'

'What's wrong with her?'

'Fiona Lee? Everything. She's one of those people who are full of book knowledge and no good at practical procedures – she can't even set up a drip properly. Another thing, she's only got to flutter her eyelashes in Longley's direction and he'll forgive her anything, whereas if I get anything wrong, he's down on me like a ton of bricks. I get it both ways; Longley compares me unfavourably with Fiona and if Doctor Melrose had her way, there wouldn't be any men working in hospitals at all.'

'She's as bad as that?'

'Every bit. In her book, men are uncaring, selfish, arrogant and aggressive and that's just for starters.'

'What did she think of Father Carey?'

'Hated him. She thought him a fool and she doesn't hold with religion, particularly Catholicism.'

'Why's that?'

'Men – again! She sees Rome as the embodiment of male privilege; contraception and abortion are two of her particular hobby-horses – she thinks that women should have absolute control over their own bodies. The continuing debate in the Anglican communion about women priests and bishops is another of her pet themes. I'm fed to the back teeth with it; she knows perfectly well that her constant attacks on the Catholic church upset me a lot.'

'How did Father Carey react to her?'

'Much as he did to everything else – with a series of jokes, many of which were pretty coarse, except during his sermon, when he let her and pretty well everyone else have it.'

'What did he say about her?'

'Just that organized religion, apart from its fundamental truth, gave a lot of people, specially those who were ill in both mind and body, a great deal of comfort, and it wasn't up to doctors, who, he had presumed in his innocence, to be working to the same end, to mock it.'

Pentland took advantage of the arrival of the wine list to glance at the young woman opposite him. Not having had much to eat all day, the gin had made him feel lightheaded and that wasn't all of it. All the feelings he had thought he had managed to banish were bubbling to the surface again. As he watched, she dug her spoon into the avocado pear in front of her and he just saw the tip of her tongue as she licked her lips in anticipation of the taste. Was there anything doing and if there was, was this the opportunity to get rid of his frustrations once and for all? She was young and attractive, looked fresh and innocent and yet surely must know her way around and this time there would be no problems unlike the disastrous occasion when . . .

Half an hour later, when he had drunk practically the entire contents of the bottle of burgundy, he began to feel sorry for himself, knowing that not only had he not the first idea about how to make an approach, but that however wholesome she might look, a woman of experience might be harbouring any one of several unpleasant social diseases, the thought of which terrified him. Carey had been right; casual sex and one-night stands were not for him and never would be.

'Your job must play havoc with your social life.'

Pentland tried to get the policewoman into focus and reached out unsteadily for the second bottle of wine, spilling a few drops on the tablecloth as he refilled his glass.

'It does.'

His social life! That was a joke. He had thought that his talk with Carey had exorcised the devil in him, but it clearly hadn't and he felt the tears rolling down his cheeks.

'What's upsetting you so much? Why not tell me about it?'

The voice was reassuring, the hand on his soft and comforting and it all began to come out.

Richard Pentland hadn't wanted to go to the leaving party for Rachel Potter, one of the staff nurses, who had been a popular member of the ITU team for five years, but everyone else would be there and he really had no choice but to do so. The party was held in one of the sitting-rooms in the nurses' hostel and to start with was a staid affair, but once Doctor Longley, Doctor Melrose and Sister Mountfield had gone, the drink began to flow more freely and most of the lights were extinguished.

Pentland was one of the few who hadn't paired off and he sat in a corner, half disgusted and half excited by what was going on. The one he couldn't take his eyes off was Liz Fletcher, Rachel's successor. She was dancing, if one could have called it that, with Bill Parker, one of his fellow registrars, and as he watched, the man's hands, which had been playing a scale between her shoulder blades, descended lower and lower until they began to creep under the hem of her very short dress. How could he, Pentland asked himself? The man had only been married for six months and here he was…. He saw the young woman give a shiver, she whispered something in his ear and then the two of them slipped out of the room.

Pentland had never even begun to come to terms with sex; as an only child of elderly parents, he had been to a series of all male boarding-schools, the last of which was run by Jesuits, and when he arrived at medical school, he felt completely lost as far as women were concerned. He had never played with girls as a child, never been out with one on his own and had completely missed out on the simplest of physical contacts with them as an adolescent. Sex instruction at his school had also been as good as useless; biologically orientated, it had answered none of his questions and, being both shy and prim, he had been left out of the 'bicycle shed' confidences that most of the other boys indulged in. Driven to extremes of anxiety and guilt at his thoughts and fantasies, he was never able to behave naturally with the female medical students and nurses, who considered him odd, and, as a result, he failed completely to develop any sort of relationship with them. He coped as best he could by throwing himself into his work and what free time he had was spent tinkering with his sports car and listening to his large collection of classical recordings.

For a lot of the time, he was able to put sex out of his mind, but often enough he was incapable of thinking of anything else, even being tortured by the sight of female patients. That had been one of the reasons why his spell in the ITU had been something of a relief; at least in that situation the patients were all seriously ill and he was able to look at them as just very sick people and nothing more than that. Such a satisfactory state of affairs didn't extend to the female staff. Jacquie and Liz ignored him, but despite that he was still tortured by them. God, he thought, how pathetic could he get? One of them only had to brush against him and he felt as if he had been scalded. He took a gulp out of the glass of wine, put it on the table beside himself, looked round at the others all of whom seemed to have paired up and struggled to his feet, being unable to bear it any longer.

'Do you think you could help me back to my room? I don't feel at all well.'

Pentland looked up to see Sister Garrard standing in front of him. He disliked the stiff and prim woman intensely, but even in the half-light he could see that she was as pale as a ghost and when he took her hand to steady her, it felt cold and clammy.

'Silly of me, I came over faint.'

'Don't you think you ought to lie down?'

'No, I'll be all right once I get back to my room and I don't want to make a fool of myself here.'

Once they were outside, she leaned against him and he helped her into the lift and up to the top floor where her flat was situated. He had never been in one of them before and took in at a glance the sparsely furnished living-room, which led off the small lobby inside the front door.

'Can I get you a hot drink, tea or something?'

Pentland had absolutely no inkling of what was about to happen, not experiencing the merest hint of anxiety about being alone with a young woman, merely feeling concern that she was so obviously unwell. He hurried into the kitchen, put on the kettle, found a teapot and in under five minutes knocked on the door of the bedroom.

'Come in.'

The sight that met his eyes very nearly caused him to drop the tray. Claire Garrard was lying without a stitch of clothing on, face down on the bed with her arms stretched out in the shape of a cross and, resting on her back, was a short whip made of knotted cords.

'Beat me,' she said in a hoarse whisper.

For one moment, Pentland was rooted to the spot, then pausing only to put the tray down on a chair, turned towards the door, keeping his eyes averted from the figure on the bed. He was out of the flat in a flash and tore down the corridor as if all the demons in Hell were after him; he took the stairs three at a time and didn't stop until he was back in the safety of his room.

He managed to get through the next few days somehow, hurrying through his evening rounds so that there would be less chance of meeting Sister Garrard. Whenever he got into bed, though, the day-dreaming started; there was no end to the variations he conjured up of the way that evening might have ended. He had comforted her and made gentle love to her, he had beaten her unmercifully, then raped her and there was every variation in between. He was unable to sleep properly and when it began to interfere with his work, he knew that unless he confided in someone, he was going to go mad. The decision taken, he got off to sleep easily for the first time since it had happened, but it only seemed as if a few minutes had gone by before he was woken by the telephone.

'Doctor Pentland, this is Nurse Clarke on the ITU. I'm sorry to have to disturb you, but I'm worried about Michael Donovan.'

'Is it his circulation?'

'No, there's a problem with his ventilation – I think his airway's partially obstructed.'

'All right, I'd better come down.'

He struggled into his clothes and when he had checked Donovan's chest, the monitors and the respirator and found nothing amiss with any of them, he caught sight of Claire Garrard, who was standing at the window of the sister's office looking at him. Pentland had seldom been more angry in his life; he waved the agency nurse away and strode into the office, closing the door behind him.

'Now, perhaps you'd be good enough to tell me what you're playing at?'

'I don't know what you mean.'

'You know very well what I mean. There haven't been any problems with Michael's assisted respiration right from the start and there aren't any problems with it now, whatever you may have told the agency nurse.'

'You've been avoiding me and I just wanted to say that I was sorry.'

'It's a bit late for that now. I want nothing more to do with you and you can consider yourself lucky that I haven't told the others about you. Now, get out of my way, you make me sick.'

One part of him knew that what he had said was true, she did make him feel almost physically ill, but another kept telling him that he couldn't blame her entirely for the fantasies he was having; after all, he had had others nearly as bad before. But why had she picked on him? It must be that she had divined that he was as rotten inside as she was herself. He couldn't go on as he was; killing himself would be one solution and the only other he could think of would be to confess to a priest or a psychiatrist. He rejected the idea of a psychiatrist almost immediately; he wasn't able to accept that he might be going out of his mind and, in a way, it made things easier to be thinking in terms of being possessed by an evil spirit, which carried with it the chance of exorcism and a cure.

Pentland did consider the possibility of going to some completely anonymous priest, but how could he expect someone who knew nothing about the hospital to understand? He did have reservations about Father Carey, but he couldn't help but be impressed by the way the man had managed to help Michael Donovan so much and maybe the bibulous Irish image was just a front. In the event, the priest fulfilled his wildest expectations. The man took him back to the presbytery, plied him with whiskey and gave him a gentle lecture on the futility of guilt and how he must learn by experience.

'The problem with sex, my friend, is that what people think they should be doing, what other people think they should be doing, what they would like to do and what, in fact, they are doing are all different. However, while it is true that there is a striking contrast between what the guardians of social behaviour consider to be appropriate and what is actually occurring, for most of us, upbringing and the social mores of our culture are important and if one tries to fly in the face of them, trouble will almost certainly arise. Why else do you suppose that Sister Garrard is such an unhappy and disturbed soul? She is the one you should really be feeling sorry for, not yourself.'

The registrar looked at the priest aghast. 'How did you know it was her?'

'My dear young fellow, you gave me a much clearer description than you realized; I would have recognized her a mile off, particularly when you described her pet instrument of punishment.'

'What do you mean?'

'You've no cause to be worrying your head about things like that; what you need to do is forget about poor tortured souls like her and find some nice, uncomplicated girls and start treating them as people by making friends with them. You like classical music, don't you?'

'Yes, I do.'

'Find a kindred spirit and invite her out to dinner and a concert. Share the enjoyment of the occasion and put any idea of sex, even the most basic thing such as holding hands, right out of your mind. For you, young fellow, marriage is what will make sex work, not furtive fumblings in parked cars, one night stands, or trying out unusual variations with disturbed young women.'

'But I can't think of anyone I could possibly ask and even if I could and plucked up enough courage to do so, they'd never agree to come out with someone like me.'

'Why do you always put yourself down like that?

You're not a bad-looking fellow, you're in a fine profession, you've got brains and you can't be badly off – that's a pretty good beginning. Tell me, who is the nicest woman you've met in the hospital?'

'Sister Mountfield.'

'You didn't have to think when you replied, did you? That means your response was genuine and there's your answer.'

'She's so old and probably doesn't like classical music.'

'She's no older than you, thirty-two to be precise, and I also happen to know that she sings in the local Bach choir – she told me so at last year's Christmas party.'

'But I wouldn't know how to set about it?'

'Simplicity itself. You'll buy a couple of tickets for a concert at the Royal Festival Hall and book a table for dinner beforehand at one of the restaurants there on a night you both have off and then you'll write her a little note.'

'But what shall I say?'

'You're the one taking her out, you know. You'll think of something.'

To Pentland's surprise, it all went off like clockwork. When he rang the box office, he found that the young Russian winner of the Leeds International Piano Competition was playing Brahms' Second Concerto in three weeks' time, Pamela Mountfield wrote back to say that she would be delighted to come and they had a thoroughly enjoyable evening. The conversation flowed, she knew as much, if not more, about music than he did and thoughts of sex, or how the evening might finish, never even raised their heads. As a result, it ended as naturally as it had begun and her warm note of thanks rounded it off perfectly.

Pentland's euphoria lasted well into the following

week; Claire Garrard kept right away from him; he had
had a brief and cheerful conversation with Father Carey
one evening after he had been visiting Michael and,
wonder of wonders, Longley had even praised his presen-
tation of a difficult case. That evening, he was sitting in the
ITU writing up some case notes, whistling quietly, when
he suddenly sat bolt upright at the sound of the high-
pitched and angry voice, which carried through the
partition between the doctors' and sister's office.

'You're drunk and there are things I know about you,
too. You're a disgrace to the priesthood and I'll have you
thrown out of the hospital.'

'I may be drunk, but at least I don't take my anger and
frustration out on patients.'

'And what is that supposed to mean?'

'You may remember that I asked you to tell Michael that
I had to go to Ireland suddenly and you chose not to do so,
causing him great distress.'

'What distress? You're making it all up – you know very
well that he can't speak and it's your drunken imagination
again.'

'And are all the other things you've been up to just in
my imagination as well?'

'Has someone been talking to you?'

'Who talks to me here and what they say are just
between them and me, as is our little talk this evening and
what you think people might have said about you is your
conscience speaking.'

'If you utter so much as a single word about me to
anyone, I'll—'

'Don't say anything you'll regret later. You're in need of
help, Claire Garrard, and as I'm clearly incapable of
providing it, I suggest you find someone else who is.'

Richard Pentland went to the door and opened it a crack as he heard the heavy tread of the priest walking along the corridor. He wasn't able to see the man, but what he did see was Claire Garrard's face and the expression on it as she followed the man with her eyes. Pentland shrank back, holding his breath and praying that she wouldn't come in, then slowly let it out as the sound of her footsteps receded.

'Why have you been telling me all this?'

Pentland looked up, trying to bring the young woman's face into focus. What was she going on about? Why wouldn't she leave him to sleep in peace? It was as bad as being woken by Sister Garrard in the middle of the night. Sister Garrard! He could see the expression on the woman's face as she followed Carey along the corridor with her eyes as clearly as on the evening when it happened.

'Because that woman is evil and when I heard that Father Carey had been poisoned, I knew at once that she was the one to have done it.'

It took Sarah the best part of an hour and a half to get Richard Pentland back to his room. When he had slumped forward on to the table in the restaurant, he wasn't just asleep, he was virtually unconscious. With the help of a couple of men, it proved easy enough to get him into his car and drive him back to the hospital, but once there her problems really started. At first, she wasn't able to rouse him, then, when she did so by using his handkerchief to squeeze some water from a puddle down his neck, he began to sing. She was able to drive to the far end of the car park before he got too raucous; it was a good hundred yards from the nearest building and there was no way he was going to be able to walk that sort of distance and, in any case, she had no idea where his room was.

There were many occasions during the next hour when she almost decided to leave him to sleep it off in the car, but decided that that wouldn't be fair. She had been the one to ply him with sufficient drink to get him to talk and from what she heard and seen of Doctor Longley, Pentland's career would not exactly prosper if the physician got to know about it. And so she sat with him in the car, talking to him, shaking him at intervals, refusing to let him go to sleep again until he was sufficiently sober to tell her where his room was. At least, then, she was able to drive right up to the side door and once there, found the key on the bunch in his pocket of his jacket.

Even when, just before one o'clock, she finally got him up the stairs and on to his bed, miraculously without waking anyone up, her problems weren't over. After she taken off his shoes, she bent forward to cover him with a blanket and was just beginning to straighten up when he made a grab for her. Her immediate instinct was to fight him off, but that only made him grip her more tightly and when she realized that all he wanted to do was give her a hug, she let him do so until gradually the tension went out of him. Within minutes, he was fast asleep and she was able to free herself.

The temptation of Pentland's car outside was too much for her – the prospect of having to make her way back to the flat at that time of night was not something she relished – so she got into it and drove home. It was knowing that she would have to return it in the morning almost as much as what Pentland had told her about the night sister that finally forced her into the decision to follow Claire Garrard. Inevitably it would mean leaving her father again, but at least there were plenty of provisions in the freezer and the weekly wash would have to wait until Sunday. She wrote him a note, set her alarm for 6.30 and then climbed into bed.

CHAPTER SEVEN

After leaving Pentland's car keys with a note in his pigeon-hole in the front hall of the hospital, Sarah was outside the nurses' home by 7.30, determined not to miss Claire Garrard should the night sister decide to leave early and go by train. The wait was not unpleasant; even though there was an autumnal nip in the air, it was warm enough to sit outside and there was even a convenient wooden seat for her to use within sight of the building. On a normal working day, she was quite sure that she would have been embarrassingly conspicuous sitting there at that time of the morning, but, being a Saturday, there was no one about other than a down-and-out sleeping under a pile of news-papers on the seat opposite her. There were a couple of empty wine bottles on the ground beside him and all she could see of him was a pair of boots with a hole in the sole of one of them, the back of a greasy overcoat and a shock of matted grey hair. What had brought him down to this level, she wondered, and what was gong to happen to him during the coming winter?

Any further speculation was cut short by the sight of the figure coming down the steps of the nurses' home. Had Michael not told her about the woman's limp, or even if there had been a lot of people about, Sarah doubted very much if she would have recognized the night sister. She had on a navy-blue coat, her hair was covered by a scarf and with dark glasses on, she might have been anyone.

As she watched the woman from the seat several rows behind on the coach as it started down M4, Sarah didn't think she had ever seen anyone sit quite so still for so long. In the half-hour that the journey had taken so far, not once had the woman looked out of the window and she kept her head bent, studying the book on her lap with intense concentration. Long before the bus had reached Exeter, Sarah was regretting having set out on the journey, being sure that Pentland had been exaggerating, and her mood wasn't improved by the teasing of the constable who met her in the unmarked Ford Fiesta.

'You want to look out for 'er,' he said in his Devonian burr, when he came back from the ticket office to say that the woman had bought a return for the bus to Cranbury. 'She looks right dangerous does your murder suspect.'

'Where is Cranbury?'

''Bout ten mile away. Lot of sinister goings in some of these out of the way villages – you wouldn't credit it. Only last week, Colonel Harvey 'ad 'is prize marrow stolen from 'is greenhouse the day before the competition.'

'What exciting lives you must lead!'

'That we do, m'dear,' he said, giving her a cheeky grin.

Sarah wasn't in the mood for that sort of badinage and was distinctly relieved when the bus they were following pulled up in the centre of the village and Claire Garrard got out, looked around and then walked across to a wooden bench in the shade of a large oak tree on the green and began to read her book again.

Sarah spent the next hour in the pub on the other side of the square, keeping an eye on the night sister from a table in one of the windows and enjoying a ploughman's lunch and a glass of cider. She had managed to part on good terms with the constable by the simple expedient of thanking him and standing him a drink at the bar, and she also discovered from the landlord that there was a village policeman in Cranbury, who lived a couple of hundred yards up the road. By now, it was quite warm, but the woman outside kept her coat and head scarf on and apart from eating some sandwiches, which she took out of her shoulder bag, she hardly moved.

'You don't come from these parts, do you?'

Sarah turned to see a florid-faced man, wearing a blazer and light-coloured slacks, bearing down on her with a large gin and tonic in his hand.

'No, I don't.'

'Come for the funeral, have you?'

Sarah grunted and looked out of the window, but the man wasn't the type to be discouraged.

'Can I get you the other half?'

There was no one else in the bar and Sarah had an instinct that he would stick to her like a leech if given half a chance.

'No, thank you. I've got to go.'

'Would you like a lift anywhere? I've got the motor outside.'

'I'm going to the ladies', if you must know.'

Sarah didn't give him the opportunity to say anything further, gathering up her coat and bag and going out through the door by the side of the bar. She wasn't going to risk finding the man waiting outside the cloakroom for her and walked straight past its entrance and out into the car park at the back. It took her no more than three minutes to get into the square again, well away from the pub, but even so, when she glanced in the direction of the tree, the seat was empty and Claire Garrard was nowhere to be seen. Sarah let out a curse under her breath; to have come all this way and then to have lost track of the woman all because of some gin-swilling Romeo old enough to be her father, was just typical of her luck.

Sarah very much doubted if Claire Garrard had noticed her at all on the coach, but, not wanting to take any risks, as she had been bare-headed then, she put on her hat and for the next ten minutes wandered round the village, but there was no sign of her quarry. Surely, she thought, if the night sister had been coming to see someone, she would have gone straight there rather than waiting in the square for an hour. The sight of the village church reminded her of what the man in the pub had said; was it possible that the woman was going to a funeral? Sarah reversed her coat so that the dark side was facing outwards and walked through the churchyard, having a last look round as she stood in the porch. No one was in sight and she opened the door cautiously, pushing aside the heavy curtain which was hanging from a circular rail around it.

'Excuse me!'

Sarah gave a violent start and took an involuntary step backwards.

'I'm so sowwy, I didn't mean to fwighten you.'

Even though the inside of the church wasn't all that dark, the contrast with the bright sunlight outside was such that she was only just able to make out the curious-looking man, but just how curious only became apparent when she had adjusted to it. At first sight, he didn't seem to be as short as all that, but that was on account of a mass of untidy, curly hair, which stood up a good four inches above his large head, but without that he wouldn't have topped five feet. Just as remarkable was his astonishing beard, which all but obscured his mouth, the high-pitched voice that emerged from it and his complete inability to say his rs properly.

'I'm Martin Irving. Uncle Gewald wanted an usher and I thought I'd get here in good time.' He peered at her through his thick glasses. 'You don't look as if you come from Cwanbuwy.'

'No, I don't.'

'I know – you must be one of Anna's fwiends, but I think Uncle Gewald might be upset if he knew that, you see....' He looked over his shoulder as he heard footsteps outside. 'I know, you can pwetend to have come with me. What's your name?'

'Sarah Prescott.'

'Why don't you sit down there, then, Sawah, and you'll get a good view.'

What on earth had tempted him into such an extraordinary deception, Sarah wondered, as she watched the little man strutting around self-importantly, showing the very sparse congregation to their places? He kept glancing in her direction, nodding his head with excitement, and she had a strong suspicion that he had never in his life had a girlfriend. She hardly needed his whispered 'Uncle Gewald' when the slim, alert-looking man with the military bearing, trim white moustache and piercing blue eyes came in and it was only too obvious that from the look he gave his nephew that the man held precious little brief for him. Sarah could only imagine that there must have been something seriously amiss with Martin's development immediately he pointed out the couple directly behind his uncle as being his parents, both of them being taller than average.

'I think you did that very well,' Sarah whispered, when the little man sat down beside her.

'Did you weally?'

'Yes, I did.'

The smile he gave her transformed his face and from then on he kept shooting glances in her direction as if to assure himself that she wasn't making fun of him.

'She was cut down in the prime of life, as if a careless woodsman had felled a sapling with a casual blow of his axe, but we all know that the great Woodsman on high in His compassion and wisdom will....'

Out of the corner of her eye, Sarah saw the curtains by the door twitch and during the next five minutes, while the vicar was in full spate, she caught occasional glimpses of the figure, who from time to time parted them a fraction. While the last hymn was being sung, she heard a faint click from the door and when, a little later, the curtains were drawn back, there was no one there. Sarah had been hoping to slip away, but there was no escaping Martin, who clung to her like a limpet and escorted her to the graveyard.

'You'll come back for a cup of tea, won't you, Sawah?' he asked, when the ceremony was finally over. 'Evewyone else will be there.'

'But what about your uncle and parents?'

'You could say you were my fwiend from the bookshop where I work in Exeter.'

The little man was pleading with her with his eyes and she didn't have the heart to refuse. Sarah didn't like the look that Colonel Irving gave her one bit when they were introduced later on; his gimlet eyes sized her up and were obviously puzzled by what they saw. Luckily, before she was subjected to an inquisition, Martin stepped in.

'Extwaordinawily moving service, didn't you think, Uncle Gewald?' he said. 'I had tears in my eyes pwactically the whole time, particularly when Father was weading the lesson. You weally wead it awfully well, Father.'

Irving's thin lips came together like a rat trap and he glanced towards his brother.

'Excuse me for a moment, would you, Henry? I see that the vicar is all on his own.'

Martin didn't appear to have noticed anything and as his parents also moved away, he picked up a plate from a nearby table.

'Why not have one of Beatwice's scones?' he said. 'They're absolutely delicious.' He pointed towards the elderly woman, who was dispensing tea from a couple of enormous silver pots. 'She's been with the family for years and to tell you the twuth, I'm fwightened to death of her, but she certainly knows how to cook and I don't know what Uncle Gewald would do without her, Aunt Elaine being the way she is.'

Sarah glanced across at the woman sitting by herself in a corner of the large sitting-room.

'Isn't she well?'

'She may look all wight, but she doesn't even know what day of the week it is. Uncle Gewald is awfully good with her; he takes her all over the place, on the golf course, to those Hellenic cwuises he so enjoys and last year they even went to Afwica. The one good thing is that she never does anything embawwassing – she just sits quietly all the time, not saying anything.'

'How sad. What's the cause?'

'Degenewation of the bwain, I believe. There's nothing anyone can do about it; Uncle Gewald has taken her to sevewal neuwologists.'

When Sarah came to look at the woman more closely, she realized that she wasn't reacting to anything going on around her, merely sitting there with a blank expression on her face, constantly twisting her fingers around. As Sarah watched, Irving went across, put a sandwich into her hand and without a word, she put it into her mouth and began to eat like an automaton.

'What a dreadful thing! Has she been ill for long?'

'She's only been as bad as this for the last few months, but it must have started about five years ago and that was why Uncle Gewald had to wetire early fwom the service.' The man took a bite out of a chocolate éclair and a large blob of cream shot out and landed on his beard. 'If you ask me,' he said, wiping it away carefully with a paper napkin, 'it was all bwought on by—'

'Martin, would you fetch your mother another cup of tea, please?'

'Of course, Father, wight away.'

Sarah took the opportunity to find the bathroom of which she was urgently in need. There was a series of doors leading off the corridor on the first floor of the house and to her dismay, the first one she tried turned out to be that to a large cupboard, which was so full that some of the contents spilled out on to the carpet as she opened it. Terrified that Colonel Irving might come up and find her there, she pushed everything back, but the door obstinately refused to shut until she discovered that a very wide framed photograph of a school group, which had slipped sideways, was causing the obstruction. She just had time to see the heading 'St Ursula's Convent School – 1995' on it before pushing it clear and closing the door.

Sarah got back into the sitting-room to find Martin

looking round anxiously and his face lit up when he saw her.

'Sorry about that, I just had to slip out for a moment.'

'Slip out?'

'The bathroom.'

The little man was overcome with confusion and moved from one foot to the other in his embarrassment. 'I'm tewwibly sowwy, I—'

'This looks delicious,' Sarah said quickly, taking a bite out of the scone, which was topped by a large dollop of clotted cream and raspberry jam. 'Mmm – excellent.'

It was so good, in fact, that she ate another before remembering her resolve to lose weight.

'No, I really mustn't,' she said, when he handed her a plate on which were slices of home-made chocolate cake.

'Go on.'

The crisp, dark icing and the thick layer of cherry jam between its two halves was almost too much for her willpower, but she managed to shake her head and patted her stomach with a rueful smile.

'I think,' he said, after gravely considering the matter, 'that you look just wight as you are.'

He was so transparently sincere that Sarah felt it was one of the nicest compliments she had ever been paid, but all thought of that evaporated when she caught sight of Colonel Irving across the room, who appeared to be scanning the guests with his sharp eyes.

'You wouldn't be able to give me a lift back to Exeter, would you, Martin? I have a train to catch and I don't think your uncle would be at all pleased if he found out that I didn't work with you.'

Sarah never did discover if his ready agreement to her suggestion was due to relief at escaping from an inquisition from his uncle, or the prospect of being alone with her in the car – probably, she thought later, it was a bit of both. At all events, he managed their departure quite skilfully, selecting a moment to say goodbye to Colonel Irving just when the vicar was hovering, obviously with the same intention.

'Goodbye, my dear Irving, the Lord moves in mysterious ways....'

The man's sonorous voice came floating across the room and, glancing backwards, Sarah could see that the parson was in full flow, his long neck bent forwards like a benign vulture.

'Why not wait for me in the car? It's not locked. I must say goodbye to Beatwice.'

The little man joined her a few minutes later and they started on their journey. Martin Irving clearly had the greatest difficulty in both reaching the pedals and in sitting high enough to see through the windscreen, but he nevertheless drove the Mini competently enough, albeit with exaggerated caution, much to the fury of a man in a large Ford estate car, which followed them along the country lanes for several minutes, flashing his headlights at intervals before overtaking them dangerously on a bend. She saw the foxy-looking face topped by a flat cap turn angrily in their direction and then he had to swerve violently to avoid hitting an oncoming tractor, scraping the side of the car against the thorn hedge. The Ford came to a screeching halt fifty yards ahead of them, smoke coming from its tyres, and by the time Martin had pulled up, the man was already striding towards them. Sarah was out of the Mini almost before it had come to a halt.

'Have you seen one of these before?' she said, showing

him her warrant card. The man, who had opened his mouth to say something, abruptly closed it again. 'May I see your driving licence, please?'

She took the greatest pleasure in putting him through the wringer; she took down his address, inspected his insurance certificate and then bent down to look at the tread on the tyres, making clicking noises with her tongue when she did so. When she straightened up, the man's temper finally got the better of him.

'If you think I'm going to be made to wait here any longer by a chit of a girl like you, you've got another think coming.'

Sarah looked at the man straight in the eye. 'You,' she said slowly and very distinctly, 'are a stupid, arrogant bully and you're a danger on the road. The tyres on your car are practically bald, one of your brake lights isn't working and, should you wish to argue the toss, you can come with me to the station in Exeter and we'll see what you register on the breathalyser. As it is, you'll report there next week with your vehicle in proper order. Is that quite clear?' The man's face was a picture, having gone from dull red to a deep purple. 'I asked if it was clear.'

She watched the Ford out of sight and then got back into the Mini beside Martin, who looked at her in admiring amazement.

'I say, you certainly gave him what for.'

'I can't stand bullies.'

Luckily for her, Martin needed all his concentration to drive and didn't comment further, but as they approached the outskirts of Exeter, Sarah saw her chances of finding out anything further about the Irvings rapidly receding.

'It was very sad about Anna, wasn't it?'

As she turned to look at him, she saw him nod and then glance in her direction.

'I don't mean to be wude, but I don't understand how you came to be fwiendly with Anna.'

'Why ever not?'

'The dwugs. I don't believe that a person like you could possibly be mixed up in anything like that.'

'Drugs?'

'Yes, I overheard Father talking to Uncle Gewald about it when the news of Anna's death came thwough.'

'I was at school with her.'

The man's face broke into a smile. 'That explains it – I just knew that you weren't that sort of person. You must also have known Claire, too. I never liked Anna – she used to make fun of me – but Claire was weally nice.'

'Why wasn't Claire here?'

'Didn't you know? There was a family wow a long time ago and Uncle Gewald wefused to see her again.'

'What was it about?'

'Something to do with weligion, but nobody told me the details.'

Even though she tried to press him, Martin wasn't prepared to say anything more about it and in any case was fully occupied with the task of negotiating the traffic at the entrance to St David's station. He gave her a little bow as they shook hands on the pavement outside.

'It was a weal pleasure to meet you,' he said.

'It was just the same for me. Thank you for the lift and for looking after me so well.'

The little man beamed at her, brought his left hand from behind his back and thrust the plastic box at her before scuttling off. Sarah waited until the car had disappeared and then opened it. The thick slice of chocolate cake had been carefully wrapped in greaseproof paper and by its side was a visiting card with Martin's name and address neatly printed on it.

Sarah fervently hoped for the girls' sake that the fearsome Mother Griselda wasn't as severe as she looked. Not once in the mercifully short interview did the headmistress of St Ursula's Convent, or whatever her correct title was, allow a smile to cross her pale and sharp-featured face, which was framed by a black headdress. She also found the woman's method of walking distinctly unnerving; in fact, she didn't appear to walk at all, she proceeded across the highly polished parquet floor, her feet invisible under long habit, almost as if she was a robot propelled by a silent electric motor.

'I don't know why you felt it necessary to come here on a Sunday,' she said, with a disapproving sniff. 'You say that this young woman died from an overdose of drugs.'

'That's right.'

'And what, might I ask, has that to do with St Ursula's?'

'Nothing directly at all. I just wanted to speak to someone who knew her when she was a pupil here. I'm trying to find out as much as I can about her background.'

'I'll make some enquiries.'

Sarah was left alone, sitting in an uncomfortable upright chair in the sparsely furnished room, for the best part of forty-five minutes before Mother Griselda came back.

'This explains it,' she said, holding up a leather-bound register. 'Anna Irving was one of the non-Catholic girls here at that time.'

'I was wondering about that.'

'About what?' the woman said sharply.

'What a non-Catholic girl was doing at a boarding convent school.'

'Well might you ask! I did not approve of having non-Catholics here and that was one of the first changes I made on taking over as principal. I would have recognized her name instantly if she had been one of my girls.' Mother Griselda let out an almost inaudible sigh. 'You'd better speak to Miss Hatfield, she was the girl's form mistress at the time she left. I can spare her for half an hour.'

Joan Hatfield was a plump woman in her early forties and Sarah's first impression was that she was quiet and diffident, but she proved to be quite the opposite. She caught Sarah's eye as Mother Griselda sailed majestically out of the room and although the two of them managed to contain themselves for a few moments, they then both burst into fits of the giggles.

'She's not as terrifying as she looks – at least not quite.'

That sally set them off again and Sarah suddenly had the daunting thought that the fearsome Mother Griselda might have heard them and be coming back. Exactly the same idea had obviously occurred to Miss Hatfield and with a tremendous effort both of them managed to get control of themselves.

'You want to know about Anna Irving? Goodness me, that takes me back, it must be all of ten years since she left. Like me, Mother Katherine, who was principal at the time, would have been very sorry to hear about her death, but although it's an awful thing to admit, I can't say that I'm all that surprised to hear that she got involved in the drug scene – she gave us all a packet of trouble.'

'Trouble?'

'If Mother Griselda had been here then, I'm sure she would have said that she was a rotten apple and would have expelled her. She wasn't such a bad girl, though, just high-spirited. She should never have been sent to a school like this and I think that even Mother Katherine might have asked her father to take her away had it not been for Claire.'

'Her sister?'

'That's right.'

'Why were two non-Catholic girls sent here?'

'We did take a few in those days. The school had and still has a great reputation for hard work and discipline, which is why Colonel Irvine wanted his daughters to come here as boarders while he was doing a tour of duty in Washington. He said that they were both in need of a firm hand and he didn't think that America would be good for them.'

'What sort of things did Anna get up to?'

'Oh, she brought some cider into the school and several girls in her dormitory were found the worse for it; she was found once doing a striptease and other things I don't like to mention after lights out, and then, almost the last straw, she went out to meet the gardener's boy one night and Anna being Anna, she was literally caught in the act, so to speak.' The woman blushed and got another fit of the giggles. 'We tried everything, lines, detention, keeping her in the sick bay with just bread and water for a day or two; once she was even given a severe strapping, but that was a mistake, it merely made her even more of a heroine to the others. Needless to say a great deal of prayer was also expended on her, but like everything else it failed miserably. To all our collective relief she left early when she was just sixteen.'

'What caused that?'

'The colonel took her away because of Claire's decision to become a nun.'

'A nun?'

'Yes, and after long thought and prayer, Mother Katherine supported her. There was the most terrible scene when Colonel Irving came to the school, with him shouting and bellowing, Mother Katherine being calm and serene as always and as for poor Claire, he slapped her across the face and told her that she was no longer a daughter of his. He went on and on; how the convent had betrayed his trust in them, that they had brain-washed her and put pressure on her to change her religion and so on.'

'How did Mother Katherine react to that?'

'She told him that she understood his anger, that she forgave him for the things that he had said and that he must understand that it was the will of God. I'm sorry to say that that only served to make him even more angry.'

'I can't say that I'm surprised to hear that. Did he try to take Claire away with him?'

'He certainly did, but she refused to go; she was eighteen and he couldn't force her. He stormed out with Anna, and Claire went off to the Provincial House of the Community of the Suffering of Christ in Northumberland. I've often wondered what happened to Claire; it was and still is a very strict order, you know, and I, for one, felt that she had the wrong personality for it.'

'In what way?'

'I suspect that one of her motives was to escape from her father. Anna once told me a bit about it; he had always wanted a boy, despised Claire for her physical disability – she had a congenital dislocation of the hip, which gave her a limp – and they never got on. He was in the habit of beating her, which was in marked contrast to Anna, whom he never touched, even though she was a tomboy and was always getting into scrapes. Anna said that Claire used to provoke him into doing it and lived in a fantasy world as the brutally treated martyr – hardly the sort of person best suited to an order like the Community of the Suffering of Christ.'

'Did you believe what Anna told you?'

'Oh, yes. I once caught Claire having put stinging nettles inside her vest while she was reading a highly coloured account of the tortures inflicted on some of the saints in a book from our library. Mother Katherine thought that she might prove incapable of submerging the self in the way required by the order, but I must admit that I was more worried by the other thing. We both tried to persuade her to join a less demanding order, but Claire wasn't to be persuaded. As she said to me, one of the main reasons she had found her true vocation was because of Mother Katherine's example and if a gentle person like her had been able to endure the strict training, then so would she. I did ask Mother Katherine once how Claire was getting on, but she either wouldn't or couldn't say.'

'How did the two sisters get on?'

'Not at all well, I'm afraid. As I said, Anna had always been her father's favourite, being athletic, physically brave and adventurous, and on her side, she thought her sister was a goody-goody, always sucking up to the teachers and Mother Katherine in particular, an opinion shared by most of the other girls. In her own way, though, Claire was extremely tough and took all the teasing and tricks without ever losing her temper and she was very brave in front of her father on that awful day – he certainly terrified me. I don't think—'

The woman stopped in mid-sentence as she heard the knock on the door.

'Yes, Louise, what is it?'

'I'm sorry to disturb you, Miss Hatfield, but Mother Griselda would like to see you.'

'All right. Thank you, Louise.'

'She did say right away.'

The woman raised her eyebrows slightly and got to her feet, giving Sarah an apologetic shake of the head.

'Don't worry, I have to get back to London in any case and I expect that Louise would show me out.'

The schoolmistress's relief was all too obvious as she hurried out of the room and Sarah noted with amusement that the girl had come in precisely thirty minutes after Mother Griselda had left.

'What's it like here?' Sarah asked the girl in the dark green pullover and skirt, as they reached the forecourt of the large stone building.

'I'm sorry. Mother Griselda told me not to discuss the school.'

Sarah was about to ask if she was being serious, when, over the girl's shoulder, she caught sight of the figure in the black headdress looking out of one of the front windows and decided that she most definitely was.

CHAPTER EIGHT

It had been Tyrrell's experience that senior physicians, such as Clifford Longley, had the knack of recruiting and retaining a certain type of middle-aged and dedicated women as their secretaries. To his considerable surprise, though, when he went to the man's office to arrange a time to interview him, he found a young woman who certainly couldn't have been a day over twenty, sitting at the desk in the outer room. With her delicate skin colouring and blue eyes, he was quite sure that she was a natural blonde; her golden hair, which had obviously been washed that morning, just reached her shoulders and her white silk blouse, which looked extremely expensive, may have been buttoned up to the neck, but the way it clung to the interesting shapes underneath and the freedom of movement it allowed, made it only too clear that lingerie, at least above the waist, was not part of her wardrobe.

'My name is Tyrrell,' he said, 'and I'd like to make an appointment to see Doctor Longley.'

She smiled at him, running her right hand through her hair. 'If it's a private appointment you want, sir, you'll have to go down to the rooms on the ground floor. Doctor Longley doesn't do private practice.'

'Actually, it's not a medical matter I wanted to see him

about; it's something personal and he's expecting me to call.'

The detective had the greatest difficulty in keeping his eyes on the young woman's face as she swivelled round in her chair and picked up the diary from the table by the side of the desk. She was just flicking through the pages when the communicating door to the inner office was thrown open.

'Sharon, do you know anything about—'

Longley stopped in mid-sentence when he saw the detective and it was obvious that he didn't recognize him at first, but then the penny dropped.

'I just looked in to fix a time to see you,' Tyrrell said.

'Ah, yes. Let me see, I'm fully occupied this evening and tomorrow, am I not, Sharon?'

'Yes, sir, I don't think you'll have time to fit anything else in.'

'Yes, you're right. Why not come to my house for a cup of tea on Sunday?' he said, turning towards the detective. 'My wife and I have a place in Islington. She's bound to want to work on a legal case she's heavily involved in and so after tea you'll have my undivided attention, which is more than can be said if we try to have a talk here.'

'Thank you, I'll be there. Your wife is in the legal business, is she?'

'She is indeed; she's a solicitor and, believe it or not, her speciality is medical litigation.' He gave a chuckle. 'No wonder people find it difficult to believe that I didn't institute divorce proceedings years ago.'

The girl had been trying hard not to laugh, Tyrrell was sure of it, and there was clearly some private joke going on between the two of them and it was not that difficult to guess what it was all about.

*

Clifford Longley's house was in the middle of a terrace of elegant Georgian houses and it had three floors above ground and a basement, with stone steps leading down to the small area below it. The bell was answered by a tall, slim, elegant woman, with russet hair with flecks of grey in it, who was wearing a filmy ankle-length dress. Thirty years earlier, he thought, she must have looked like one of Burne-Jones's models and was still beautiful, but with an aura of melancholy about her.

'Chief Inspector Tyrrell? Do come in, Clifford will be down directly.'

Tea, served by their housekeeper, was as elegant as his hostess with wafer-thin sandwiches and sponge cake and conversation flowed with a discussion of Alan Bennett's new play, the exhibition of Landseer paintings at the National Gallery and a recent recital by Alfred Brendel, which they had all attended.

'I see from your expression that you find it difficult to comprehend what is going on,' Longley said, when his wife had excused herself and the two men were on their own. 'I like to think that I'm a good judge of character and having discussed this at length with Angela earlier today, not only do I believe that I can trust you to keep what I am going to tell you to yourself, but we both think it better to explain the situation, rather than your hearing a no doubt garbled and over-inflated version from some "well wisher" at the hospital. Why, you must be saying to yourself, is someone with a beautiful and highly intelligent wife diverting himself with the likes of young Sharon? Well, Angela and I met at university where I was reading natural sciences and she law. We had many interests in common, saw a great deal of each other and when we came down, we got married. Sexual behaviour by the likes of us was very different in those days and it was by no means uncommon for engaged couples to confine it to hand holding and hugs and kisses and premarital innocence was not confined to women, either. Anyway, when it came to it after the wedding, it proved impossible for Angela to ... I'm sure I have no need to spell it out. She offered me an annulment, but she was precious to me and we worked out the solution that still exists today, one that was made easier owing to the fact I no more wanted children than she did. I wasn't to know then that once I had woken up to that side of life it would become almost an obsession, but that's what happened and the radical change in social mores made it easier. I was as discreet as possible in my amatory adventures away from home and have remained so in our circle of friends, but I was tempted by some of the nubile young women at the hospital and secrets are difficult to keep in places like that. In Father Carey's philosophy, I should have stayed with my wife and remained celibate. Well, I have done the former, but not the latter and we enjoy our life together in so many ways.'

'Have there not been risks of complications with regard to the other arrangements you have made?'

Longley smiled. 'Very delicately put. Yes, but if the lines are drawn up correctly right from the start and one is suitably generous, not very often, particularly if one doesn't allow love, jealousy, sexual or otherwise, to enter into it.'

'I admire your skill. What's your secret?'

'Basic talent and a good deal of practice, I suppose. In the same way that you must have developed the ability to know whether or not people are speaking the truth, and any good physician can tell at a glance if someone is really ill, I am able to sense whether a young woman is a candidate for serious endeavour or not. Subtle skills like that are difficult to analyse; I suppose it's a combination of the ability to read body language, the interpretation of tones of voice and many other much more delicate messages. Do you remember your schooldays and how you were able to recognize in a flash that there were some masters with whom you just did not try to take liberties? They had authority in a way that is difficult to define and were by no means always the strictest disciplinarians. It is rather the same with patients and their doctors; they either have confidence in them or they don't. It goes without saying that that is a very individual matter and, for example, I find some of the some physicians at St Cuthbert's arrogant and insensitive and would never consult them personally and yet they all have their devoted followers. One of the things that makes human relationships so intriguing is that they are two-way affairs and with regard to the particular variety that I am interested in, there is the added spice and exhilaration of hidden danger. In the same way as I never allow patients to become too dependent on me, the same is true of my sexual relationships. I am looking for excitement and mutual fun, pleasure and respect. I am not interested in conquest, domination or love. The most important thing is to find kindred spirits. A lot of young women aren't interested in older men, or worse, find them unattractive and even pathetic, but there are plenty of others who don't.'

'But you must make mistakes occasionally, even bad ones.'

'I did just that once and I've had to live with the consequences ever since; I've no intention of repeating it.'

Tyrrell nodded 'Now, about Father Carey: I've already

heard about his dislike of the way AIDS is handled at the hospital.'

'Carey didn't know the first thing about it. Just because I believe that AIDS is best handled in special units, he interpreted that as meaning that I think that they shouldn't be treated at all. It's all very easy to take moral stances if one is not in the front line. Quite a few doctors, nurses and laboratory workers are frightened of it and those fears have to be respected, and it's not only that, it's also a question of resources and expertise. How can St Cuthbert's possibly look after those patients properly when experience there of the condition is so limited? It's true that it is one of the greatest medical challenges of the day, even in the UK, particularly in the immigrant population, but so is cancer and our oncology unit is second to none. All I've been saying is that it's horses for courses, no more than that.'

'How come you have a patient with AIDS on the ITU, then?'

'The man in question has been attending the diabetic clinic at the hospital for years and Earnshaw, who runs that unit, insisted that the fellow be admitted. I opposed the idea, but lost the battle in committee. You can't win 'em all, you know.'

'What is Doctor Melrose's view of all this?'

'She belongs to the opposing camp, but at least, unlike some of the others, she's quite open about it. We're very lucky to have Doctor Melrose; she's immensely hard-working, very able and totally dedicated to her job, almost too much so, I believe. I've always encouraged the students to be whole people, rather than focus on medicine to the exclusion of everything else, let alone a small branch of it, but it isn't up to me to criticize other people's lifestyles and if they're happy with the situation, good luck to them. After all, I don't like people doing that to me, particularly behind my back.'

'It must be very difficult working the whole time on the ITU.'

'It is and that's why I don't do it; I also have general medical beds and clinics.'

'Did you come across Father Calvert much?'

'Hardly at all. You may have gathered already that I hold no brief for organized religion, nor its practitioners. Obviously not everyone shares that view, or if they do, are prepared to voice it, but shall I say that I merely know what he looks like. As for Carey, he practically camped out on the ITU after Donovan was admitted, so inevitably I've seen quite a bit of him recently. I like his brand of religion even less than Calvert's; the idea of men and women living lives of forced celibacy appals me. I'm prepared to concede that it works for some, but a great many others are put under intolerable strain or else cheat the system, which produces equally intolerable guilt. They're fond of saying that men and women aren't animals, but I don't know where they got that idea from; they are and very dangerous ones at that. You, for one, would be out of a job, if they weren't.'

'Do you think that Father Carey had enemies?'

'I wouldn't be surprised if he had. He drank too much and he gossiped, neither of which activities are to be recommended if people take you into their confidence. I'm not only talking about the confessional; people say all sorts of things to priests in other situations, not least in the bar if you happen to be a hail-fellow-well-met type like Carey.'

'What about one of them killing him?'

'Who knows what goes on in people's minds, or what actions they might take if they are sufficiently provoked?'

'Do you know Sister Garrard?'

'Garrard? No, the name doesn't ring any bells.'

'She's one of the night sisters and was at the Mass given for Donovan.'

'I don't have any contact with the night staff these days; I delegate the management of emergencies to the younger generation – I'm too old for that sort of thing now.'

As he drove off, Tyrrell had the distinct feeling that he had been assessed as effectively as any of Longley's young women. But had he been manipulated, too, and was what he had been told about the man's marriage true? It was a bizarre enough arrangement in all conscience and he had to admit that the man's charm and frankness had been disarming, but he still thought that he wasn't making it all up – he must have known that there was a possibility that his wife might also be questioned and Tyrrell was convinced, despite only the most fleeting acqaintance with the woman, that she wouldn't be the sort to lie about something like that. Damn it, he thought, he had even found himself liking the man and he could see why his patients might well feel the same. It was clear, though, from what Donovan had communicated to them, that he was not popular with some of the ITU staff. What would Longley make of Sarah, he wondered? Tyrrell was quite sure that even if he considered her to be forbidden fruit, his internal computer would be clicking away and would have assessed her in a flash. Attractive? Yes, certainly. Nice? Equally so. Sexual potential? Untapped, but promising. Wish for stable marriage? Probable. Prospects for dalliance with a man of mature age and with money to spend? Negligible. Ideal partner/husband? Professional man, physically active, both nice and intelligent, not too young, but under forty – rather like Michael Donovan must have been before his accident. Yes, Tyrrell thought, it was an amusing game to play, but it did tend to bring uneasy truths to the surface.

'How did you get on?

Sarah Prescott sat down in front of Roger Tyrrell's desk and took a pile of notes out of the folder on her lap.

'I saw Jacquie and Liz this morning and didn't get much out of either of them. Jacquie obviously doesn't like Doctor Longley. She thinks he's stuck up and pompous and doesn't care for the way he bullies Doctor Pentland, but is prepared to concede that the registrar is a wimp, although good at his job. She also said that she overheard Longley and Doctor Melrose discussing Father Carey's sermon and, although the two of them take a different stance on the AIDS question, they were united in their dislike of his using his privileged position to make ill-informed comments about it.'

'Michael said that Carey had hinted to him that Longley was an adulterer. Did you get any suggestion from those two young women that he might have a roving eye?'

'Well, Jacquie did say that he was a dirty old man.'

'In what way?'

'It seemed to amount to little more than his way of looking at her – he's never actually tried anything on. When I asked Liz about that she said that he had always behaved perfectly correctly with her, but I'm not so sure.'

'Why not?'

'Just a feeling I had. She didn't blush, or anything, just went quiet all of a sudden and looked away.'

'Did they have anything to say about the others?'

'Not a great deal. They respect Doctor Melrose, but

don't like her much, and had nothing but good to say about Sister Mountfield.'

'And Father Carey?'

'Both said that they hardly knew him, but thought he was wonderful with Michael.'

'And that leaves Sister Garrard.'

'Ah, yes. Sister Garrard.'

'Come on, you can't fool me; you found out something about her, didn't you?'

Roger Tyrrell listened in silence while Sarah described what had happened both with Richard Pentland and in Devon, making occasional notes on the pad in front of him and when she had finished, looked straight at her for a moment or two.

'What you did in Exeter was a great piece of work – you did very well, very well indeed. As for me, I had tea with Longley at his house in Islington.'

'What was he like?'

'I rather took to him. He's not at all the pompous, self important fellow I was expecting, but he does seem to be walking on something of a tightrope.'

'In what way?'

'Carey was right about the adultery bit, but it's not as bad as it sounds – there are distinctly unusual extenuating circumstances, which I think are best kept under wraps, at any rate for the time being. There is certainly something going on between him and his secretary – you should have seen the looks passing between them when I went to his office to make an appointment to see him. When I had a chat to him, I even wondered if the same was true about him and Claire Garrard. He claimed not to know who she was or even her name as he no longer did any night work, but he was just that little bit too quick to say so.'

'What was his view of Father Carey?'

'Dismissive would, I think, be the best way to describe it. He clearly holds no brief at all for religion or those who administer it and obviously believes that the man was indiscreet in the extreme, particularly when he was in his cups.'

'What do we do next?'

'I must clearly have a talk with Doctor Melrose, which I'll do tomorrow morning, and I wonder if you'd see Michael this evening and tell him what's happened.'

'How much of it?'

'The lot. The poor man has precious little to live for and he obviously has a burning desire to help in finding Father Carey's killer. Apart from that, I'd trust him even if he could speak. And Sarah.'

'Yes, sir.'

'I've already praised you for your excellent work in Exeter, but what you did with Pentland was indefensible.' Sarah felt the cold shiver go right down her back, but didn't lower her gaze. 'Let me spell it out. By your own account, you flirted with him, if not actively encouraging him, you did nothing to stop him drinking until he was incapable of thinking straight, you then drove him back to the hospital, put him to bed and then compounded the whole thing by using the same car to get yourself home. Do you know about the Rachel Nickell case?'

'It was mentioned in one of our lectures, sir.'

'Well then, you have no excuse for not knowing about honey traps, which was the term used by the press back in 1994 when it all happened. In that particular case, the WPC in question was ordered to ingratiate herself with the man whom her seniors were convinced had done the murder and they were the ones guilty of having set the whole thing up. All hell was let loose when it came into the public domain, but you have no such excuse. You will go down to records right now, you will look up that case, take in all the details and you'll never do anything like that again. Consider yourself lucky that you're not being suspended. Is all that quite clear and do you understand that you have been both irresponsible and foolish?'

'Yes, sir. I'm very sorry, sir.'

After supper that evening, Tyrrell was making a half-hearted attempt at doing the crossword and keeping an eye on a snooker match on TV at the same time when he saw Alison watching him. The hint of a smile and the slight raising of her eyelids was enough to convey her meaning as if she had painted it on a placard in letters two feet high.

'It's getting chilly down here, I'm bored with my book, the children are asleep and wouldn't it be more fun upstairs,' is what she conveyed.

Despite nearly fifteen years of marriage, their relationship had never drifted into the predictable and there was always some exciting and unexpected variation on both their parts to keep it alive and full of spice. He also knew with utter certainty that, superficially exciting it may have sounded when he was hearing about it, sexual adventures such as Longley's held no attraction for him at all.

His almost imperceptible nod and accompanying grin replied: 'Good idea. What have you got up your sleeve this time, you she-devil?'

'Give me twenty minutes and you're not to come up a second earlier.'

If Sarah had rung him half an hour later, he would either not have replied, or else wrung her neck the following day, but as it was her call had nothing to do with

P E T E R   C O N W A Y

the uncomfortable interview earlier that day and it even filled in the time nicely.

'Sorry to disturb you at this hour,' she said, 'but Michael would like to go down to the chapel again, if at all possible with a reconstruction of that mass. He says he's got something niggling away at the back of his mind and he believes that it might jog his memory. If you agree, I thought it would save time if you were to ask Doctor Melrose tomorrow.'

'Good idea. How was it with Michael?'

'He asked lots of questions and wants to think about the whole thing.'

'Why not take tomorrow morning off? You were working the whole weekend and you deserve a break. We might meet for lunch – twelve-thirty in the front hall of the hospital suit you?'

'Yes, sir.'

Tyrrell glanced at his watch, tiptoed up the stairs and at exactly the time agreed, threw open the bedroom door.

CHAPTER NINE

'After all that, are you sorry that you followed the Garrard woman down to Exeter?' Michael signalled, when Sarah had finished telling him about all that had happened over the weekend.

Sarah gave his hand a squeeze. 'You know I'm not, except for that business with Pentland, which was stupid in the extreme; I don't know how I'm going to face Tyrrell the next time I see him.'

'I shouldn't worry, if I were you, I have an instinct about him; I think he was right to give you a bollocking, but my guess is that it will be the last you hear of it.'

'I do hope so. It's just as well I didn't make that bet with you, though, isn't it?'

'You've changed.'

'How do you mean?'

'You suspected that that bet would have involved something sexual and you were terrified, weren't you? And look how you handled that funny little man in Devon; I won't embarrass you by mentioning Pentland.'

Sarah raised her eyebrows. 'Both Pentland and Martin Irving are lame ducks and the truth is that I'm just as lame as either of them; I haven't the first idea how to handle a relationship with men. It's not that I'm uninterested, it's just that my emotional development is at the level of a twelve-year-old and a pretty sheltered one at that.'

'Go on. I can't believe that anyone in the police force remains innocent for very long.'

'Oh, I know all the words and what goes on, but you might say that I've failed the practical. I'm ashamed to have to admit it, but I've even invented a live-in boyfriend, who's in the army and prone to violent fits of jealousy. Puerile, isn't it, but it's worked and kept the wolves at bay.'

'Sad, not puerile. How did it happen?'

'I was just twelve when my mother had her first operation for breast cancer and she died two years later. My father had married late; he had already retired when it happened and so, in effect, I became his housekeeper. It was my uncle, my mother's brother, who encouraged me to follow a career, when all my father wanted me to do was stay at home and look after him, or at best become a secretary. Why the police? Watching too many TV programmes, I suppose, and the fact that my uncle thought it was a good idea. He had some contacts, arranged for an interview and that was that. I hadn't the faintest idea what I was letting myself in for and, until last week, I would have said that I had made a terrible mistake, but now I know that I haven't and nothing is going to stop me making a success of it.'

'Not even your father?'

Sarah sighed. 'He was just about tolerable when I was doing an office job with fixed hours, but now....'

'Is he difficult?'

'God, is he difficult? If I'd been older and more mature at the beginning, I'd never have let him get away with it, but then it got into a pattern and I wasn't able to break it.

If ever I wanted to go out, he'd whine about being left alone all day while I was at school and it was too much to expect him to be on his own in the evenings as well, and I'd give in, feeling sorry for him. And then, if a school-friend, or my uncle invited me away for a night or a weekend, he would always develop some symptom or illness and that would be that. The trouble now is that I just can't do my present job and look after him as well – one or the other's got to go, that much has become only too obvious in the last couple of days. He's hopeless; he can't or won't cook, do the shopping, housework, or anything else useful for that matter. He spends the whole day reading, watching TV and doing the crossword.'

'You've got to leave him.'

'I know I have, but how?'

'What used he to do when he was working?'

'He was an accountant.'

'Get him a housekeeper. He's obviously had an unpaid one for years and if I know anything about accountants, he's bound to have pots of money salted away. As for you, the police must have hostels where you could stay until you find a place of your own. You could easily be out of your prison inside a fortnight.'

'Just like that?'

'Just like that.'

'I'll have to think about it.'

'You must do more than just thinking about it.'

'I know.'

'Cheer up, you'll find a way. Oh, Sarah, would you do something for me? No, don't worry, I'm not at it again, something perfectly straightforward.'

'Of course.'

'I have the feeling if I went down to the chapel again

with everyone present just as before, it might jog my memory. I may be wrong, but at the back of my mind there's the thought that there is a clue to be picked up and I'm sure it's worth a try.'

'Good idea. I'll give Tyrrell a ring directly I get back to the Yard. I'd rather not do it here and if I use the one at home at this time of night Father's bound to make a fuss and I've got to pick up something there in any case.'

'Are you sure it's not too much trouble and do you think it wise to, considering what happened between you and him this afternoon?'

'I think it's too important to worry about that.'

'Thanks, and perhaps it's not a bad idea to let Tyrrell know that you're not going to retreat into your shell. Good luck!'

She bent down and kissed him gently on the lips, so gently that he even thought he might have imagined it, but there was no imagination about the frantic rate of his heartbeat that had the night nurse anxiously checking it until it had settled.

It took Michael Donovan a long time to get off to sleep that night. Would Sarah have the guts to do what he had suggested? It was very easy for him to tell her to leave the old man, but that particular old man was her father. What a miserable life the poor girl must have had and how it contrasted with his own privileged upbringing. His parents, both dead now, had also been elderly and he had been an only child, too, but they had always encouraged his independence and when his father had had a fatal heart attack, his mother had refused to be a burden on him. 'Yes,' she had said, 'I know you've got plenty of room in your flat, but you wouldn't want an old woman like me descending on you for any length of time and anyway, I can manage perfectly well on my own and I don't think it would be at all sensible for me to live in London away from my friends.'

Why hadn't he had the sense to find someone like Sarah to share his life and have children while there was still time? There had been a succession of young women like Helen, who had highly paid jobs and knew exactly what they wanted both in and out of bed and where were they now? Certainly not visiting him, and like as not driving fast and competently in their GTIs to dinner dates with like-minded yuppies.

Sarah could hardly have been more different from them. She had not become cynical or defeated, despite her experiences at the hands of her father and the bully at the Yard and he sensed that a relationship with her – he felt sure that she would want it to lead to marriage – would have been infinitely more rewarding than any of the multitude of casual ones that he had had in the past. She was certainly innocent, but that didn't mean that she was naïve; she had known at once what he was after when he had mentioned a bet and she had been quite right to have had nothing to do with it. Helen would have stripped off, or done any of the other things he had in mind, without a second thought and without it meaning a thing, but if Sarah had agreed merely for pity's sake, it would have demeaned them both. He would have given all his possessions to be able to help her to leave that tyrant of a father of hers and set up on her own, but how could he do anything when he was literally unable to lift a finger?

When Sarah came out of the Yard, she waited for a minute or two on the pavement outside hoping that a taxi would come by and then, when there was no sign of one, began to walk towards Victoria Station. She had got no more than a hundred yards up the road when a white car pulled up alongside her and the passenger door was thrown open.

'Get in!'

She just had time to feel a frisson of fear before she saw that it was Terry Painter leaning across the front seat. Having spent the best part of a year working for him and doing precisely what he had told her for so long and without question, it never occurred to her to refuse.

'Fasten your seat belt!'

As she started to do so, Sarah glanced sideways at him. The man's clothes were crumpled, he obviously hadn't shaved since the previous day and even though he was staring straight through the windscreen, she could smell alcohol on his breath.

'I need your help with a little job this evening. It's all right, I've cleared it with Tyrrell. House in Hampstead's been robbed, the owners are abroad and an au pair's in charge. I have to interview her and I need to take a woman along with me.'

It didn't make sense to Sarah and she knew at once that something was wrong, very wrong. Painter would never have gone out on an enquiry in the state he was in now and Tyrrell would certainly have told her about it when she had telephoned him to ask about the arrangements for Michael's visit to the chapel. She turned abruptly to open the door, but before she had time to reach the catch, his right arm came across, slamming her back in her seat.

'I told you to fasten your belt. All right, I'll do it for you.'

Keeping his left forearm across her neck, he pulled it across her chest and when it was secure, placed his left hand firmly over the release button.

'You're coming to help me whether you like it or not

and I'm warning you, I'm not in a good mood; try to get out of the car again and you'll be on the receiving end of a bunch of fives right in the mouth.'

He didn't say another word throughout the journey; usually a fast and aggressive driver, he kept to the speed limits, respected all the red lights and all the time kept shooting glances in her direction until the car swept into a crescent-shaped drive in front of a large detached house. As soon as it came to a halt, he was out of it and round to the passenger door before she had time to release the belt. Taking her wrist in a vice-like grip, and pulling her arm up behind her back, he marched her up to the front door and pulled a bunch of keys out of his pocket. When he had unlocked and opened it, she hear the intermittent warning tone of the burglar alarm and the idea of trying to kick him, or of dropping to the ground, thereby delaying him for long enough for the alarm to go off, went through her mind, but he had obviously anticipated that, giving her arm a violent jerk, which sent an agonizing pain right through her shoulder. She stumbled over the step, fighting to maintain her balance and ease the pressure on her arm, but he kept it up relentlessly while he switched off the alarm inside the cloakroom to the left and then pushed her into a room on the opposite side of the hall. Even then, he didn't let her go until he had drawn the heavy velvet curtains across, switched on the lights and locked the door, putting the key in his pocket.

'Sit down in that armchair over there.'

Massaging her aching shoulder, Sarah did as she was told and while Painter adjusted the curtains to his satisfaction, she looked round the room. Her armchair was on one side of the ornate fireplace, a matching one was on the other side and facing it was a large three-seat sofa. Heavy brass lamp stands were on glass-topped tables on either side of it and with the thick pile carpet and three oil paintings, each with its own light above, it was obvious to her, even at that moment, that the house and contents must have been worth a small fortune.

At that moment, Painter moved across to the sofa and sat down heavily, staring at her from a distance of no more than six feet.

'You didn't believe that story I told you right from the start, did you? Do you want to know the real reason why I brought you here?'

Sarah could guess. What had the lecturer, who had given a talk on how to deal with situations like this, said? Do or say something unusual, anything to confuse or surprise your assailant.

'I asked you a question.'

The man's voice had risen both in pitch and volume and although she was trembling, Sarah forced herself to smile.

'I don't know about you, but I could do with a drink.' She pointed towards the row of decanters on the mahogany sideboard with their shield-shaped silver labels secured by delicate chains made of the same material. 'Whisky, brandy or port?'

Without looking at him, Sarah poured out a tumblerful of neat whisky and a glass of port and brought them back, putting the whisky on the table by Painter's side. As she sat down again, she saw him looking at her in blank amazement, then he picked up the glass and swallowed half the contents.

'I didn't believe that story of yours about a live-in boyfriend, but now I'm not so sure. That's all to the good – I never was that keen on reluctant virgins. I'll tell you what's going on and then you can be nice to me.'

Sarah felt her whole body tighten up and had to clench her jaws together to stop her teeth from chattering as the man downed the remainder of the whisky in his glass, then got up to replenish it.

'I don't need to tell you that I've been involved in a big drugs' investigation for some months now and just when I was getting really close to the people running it, I've been suspended.'

'Suspended? What ever for?'

'That bastard Maskell found out that I'd received a few backhanders; what he doesn't know yet, is that they came from the bloke who owns this pad. What's wrong with that? It's a dangerous business getting close to blokes like him and worth a bit extra. How else does that smug sod sitting on his backside in his warm office think we're going to catch 'em? By sticking to the rules like that smoothie Tyrrell? He's making out with you, is he? Is that why he took you away from my office?' The man shook his head and took another gulp from his glass. 'Haven't got an office now. You will be nice to me, won't you? I bet you've got some surprises under those dull clothes of yours. You wouldn't be a bad looker, you know, if you took a bit more trouble. How about giving me a preview. Take off your coat as a start.'

The man was looking at her blearily, obviously having difficulty in focusing clearly, and if only she could keep him talking, she thought, surely the amount he had had to drink would catch up with him.

'How did Maskell find out about you?'

'It must have been that bugger Pearce. It stands to reason; I never had any trouble until he came on to the scene and I reckon Maskell must have put him on to spying on me. I was waiting outside the Yard to duff him up a bit when you came out and I realized what I really needed was a bit of home comfort – Pearce can wait. I thought I told you to take that coat off.'

Sarah saw the anger in his eyes and, as he made a move to rise to his feet, got up herself, quickly refilled his glass and then slowly unbuttoned her coat, slipped it off her shoulders and put it over the back of the armchair.

'Let me look at you. Stand there in front of the fireplace and brace your shoulders back a bit. Hmm! Not bad, not bad at all. I ought to have done something about you long ago. Now, how about that blouse?'

'It was very clever of you to get hold of the keys of this house. How did you do it?'

'Took some impressions in plasticine. If you believe that, you'll believe anything. Nah, the bloke and his missus are in Spain and I'm minding the shop while they're away, even watering the plants.' He gave a cavernous yawn and peered at her with hooded eyes. 'What about that blouse, then?'

His eyes closed for a second, opened briefly as he tried to get her into focus, then his head fell to one side and he began to snore gently. Sarah stood looking at him for a full three minutes, trying to pluck up enough courage to try to find the key to the door. The trouble was that he had had his back to her when he had locked it and she hadn't seen which pocket he had put it into. She tiptoed across to the windows, but as she had feared, they were both double-glazed and locked – it would have to be the door. She was leaning over him with the fingers of her left hand poised inches above his jacket pocket, when he suddenly grabbed her wrist and pulled her down on top of himself.

'I thought your behaviour was a bit too good to be true,

darlin'. Wanted to get me incapable, did you? Nice try and I don't mind; I like a bit of a struggle.'

As she felt his lips on hers and smelled the alcohol on his breath, Sarah stretched her right hand out, feeling frantically for the heavy glass ashtray she had seen on the table. Jerking her head sideways, she saw that it was a good twelve inches away and she had almost given up hope of reaching it when he pushed her sideways, trying to force his knee between her legs. Her fingers closed over it and without taking aim, she brought it down as hard as she could.

Painter let out a bellow of pain, her wrist was released and she half rolled and half scrambled out of his reach. Massaging his damaged shoulder with his right hand, he moved his position so that he was sitting on the very edge of the sofa.

'I'm going to make you suffer for that.'

His face twisted into a grin and he suddenly hurled himself at her. His foot caught in the rug in front of the fireplace and, as she jumped sideways, he shot past her and there was a sickening thud as his head hit the marble surround and he lay there motionless. Without giving herself time to worry about whether or not he was faking again, Sarah took four sets of keys out of his pockets, those of his car, the room, the front door and what she presumed must be his own place and then stood for a moment looking round.

Every instinct was telling her to get out as quickly as possible, but even at that moment, she knew with absolute certainty what would happen if her presence in the house were to be discovered – she would also be suspended and she could only too easily imagine the rumours that would be flying around about her relationship with Painter and she had to prevent that happening at all costs. Using the man's handkerchief, she wiped the decanters, the ash tray and everything else that she could conceivably have touched, clear of fingerprints, washed the two glasses in the kitchen and after she had returned them to the sideboard, locked the door to the sitting-room behind her.

As she was on the point of making a 999 call to the police, she suddenly realized that she didn't know the address of the house, but then she saw the pile of circulars that Painter must have put on the chair by the umbrella stand on another occasion and read it out to the operator who answered her. Sarah wasn't sure whether or not all 999 calls were recorded and decided to play safe by talking through the handkerchief.

'There's an unconscious man in the locked front room to the right of the hall. I'll leave the key by the telephone in the hall and the front door will be unlocked. While you're at it, it might be worth searching the place – it's owned by a man running a drugs' syndicate.'

Sarah realized that there was a chance that there might be a patrol car in the vicinity and she had no intention of getting caught on the premises, so she hurried out to Painter's car and drove it to a side street near Hampstead underground station. It was then that the shock hit her and although there was nothing more she wanted than to get back to the safety of her bed in the flat, she began to shake uncontrollably and ten minutes went by before she was able to think clearly enough to remove any prints she might have left in the car and make for home.

Sarah looked at her watch as she let herself into the flat. Could it really only be 11.20? It seemed a lifetime since she had left the hospital. A board creaked as she crept past her father's bedroom and she paused, her heart in her mouth, knowing that she wouldn't be able to face him, or anyone else, just yet. Even though Painter had hardly touched her, she still felt dirty and, stripping off her clothes, got into the bath, with the water as hot as she could bear it.

Looking down at her body, pink and half hidden by the steam, Sarah had a sudden vision of it torn, bruised and bleeding and despite the heat, began to shiver again. If she had been raped, she knew with utter certainty that she would never be able to.... All of a sudden, in her mind's eye, she saw Michael Donovan stretched out on his bed and covered, as usual, by a single sheet.

'You weren't raped,' he signalled, 'and you weren't even injured, and there's no call to be feeling sorry for yourself. You should be proud; you didn't panic and you got so much whisky into him and then you neatly incapacitated him. And don't you dare for one minute even think of using what has happened as an excuse for failing to tackle your father.'

It acted better than a tonic; she got out of her bath, towelled herself vigorously and went to bed, sleeping deeply until her alarm went off.

Sarah waited until exactly eleven o'clock, which was the time her father liked his morning cup of coffee and a single chocolate biscuit. He was sitting in his favourite armchair in the living room in front of the large window, which gave him a view of the river and *The Times* was folded on his lap. As she came into the room with the tray, he filled in a clue in the crossword and put it to one side.

'Father, there's something important I have to say to you.'

'Not now, Sarah, can't you see that I'm busy?'

She took a deep breath, determined to keep calm. 'I

won't be able to do my present job and look after you properly – the arrangement we have at present isn't fair to either of us.'

'So you've at last deigned to notice that you've been neglecting me for the past week, have you?'

'I'm going to put an advertisement in a magazine for a housekeeper and then arrange to hold interviews with you.'

'You'll do no such thing. That ass Henry Garnett tried the same damn fool suggestion on me some time back and I soon told him where he got off.'

'That was a long time ago, Father, and I'm sorry to have to put it quite so bluntly, but either you let me help you to find someone, or else you'll have to do it on your own.'

'But I can't afford a hired help.'

'You know perfectly well that you've got plenty of money and I'm not talking about a help, I'm talking about a resident housekeeper.'

'There isn't room in this flat for a housekeeper.'

'I'm leaving, Father, just as soon as this is fixed up.'

He stared at her, obviously trying to decide whether or not she meant it.

'You can't leave me all on my own,' he whined. 'I'm not well and—'

'I won't be leaving you on your own and there's nothing wrong with you at all.'

In a flash, his expression changed. 'You're a wicked cruel girl and you're no daughter of mine.'

'Oh, come on, Father.'

'Don't call me Father, I'm not your father. You'd better sit down – I said sit down!'

His voice had risen to a shout and Sarah could see his hands shaking as he put the newspaper down. She hesi-

tated for a moment and then pulled up a chair, her deter-
mination never to be bullied by him again overcome by
her need to hear what he had to say.

'Your mother,' he said, putting undue emphasis on the
word, 'was my secretary at the firm of accountants of
which I was the senior partner, when she got into trouble,
or whatever the current euphemism is. She was an excellent worker, had been with me for ten years and I had
become very fond of her. By the time she came to me in
great distress to tell me what had happened, it was already
too late to do anything about it and, feeling sorry for her, I
decided to take her on as my wife, for better or worse. As
it turned out, it was for the worse. Had it not been for you,
we would have been happy. You always were a spoiled
brat and you've never grown out of it. If I'd had my way,
I'd have knocked some sense into you while there was still
time, but your mother was soft-hearted and that arrogant
bully of an uncle of yours stuck his oar in and— Who was
your father? Your mother wouldn't tell me, but it's
obvious that he was no good – look what he's produced.
There's nothing I can do to change you now, but if you've
been thinking that you're going to come into a pretty
penny when I'm gone, you can think again – you won't get
a brass farthing.'

Sarah could have said any number of things; that she
wouldn't accept anything from him even if he begged her
to take it, that he could stew in his own juice, that she was
leaving as soon as she could pack her things, that she
never wanted to see him again, but she said none of them,
knowing that she had to get out of the room as quickly as
possible. She saw from his expression of triumph as she
turned to leave that he thought she was going away to
have a good cry and that she would come creeping back

begging his forgiveness, but the reality was the complete opposite. She ran out of the flat and along the path by the side of the river, scarcely able to contain the extraordinary feeling of liberation that was welling up within her.

She was to think later that the psychiatrists would have had a field day with her. It was as if all of a sudden she had been given permission to hate the man who had called himself father for all those years, to hate him for his meanness, his lack of warmth, his selfishness, his everything. There was also the relief of knowing that there was nothing of him in her at all, not one gene, not a single chromosome. It wasn't only that: a mere few days of working for Tyrrell had demonstrated to her that she was able to take initiative on her own, she had dealt with Painter, and young men, admittedly all three of them flawed in one way or another, had found her attractive. What's more, she was now free to work all the time that was necessary to develop her skills and personality unfettered by that miserable old tyrant, Arthur Prescott.

When she got back to the flat, he was still sitting in the living-room facing the window and didn't turn as she spoke.

'I have to go out now. Your lunch is on the kitchen table and there's some of the casserole in the fridge for your supper in case I don't get back in time. It's already in the right dish for the microwave, I've covered it with clingfilm and made some perforations in it for you, so all you have to do is cook it for three minutes on high.'

She didn't give him the opportunity to reply, hurrying out to meet Roger Tyrrell for lunch.

CHAPTER TEN

Roger Tyrrell had taken on Sarah Prescott as his assistant for the simple reason that Commander Maskell had told him to do so. Terry Painter was in trouble, big trouble, his superior had said, which meant that Sarah Prescott was going to be out of a job and the fact that Bert Bristow had broken his leg made it the ideal solution. Tyrrell had had his reservations, not only about her, but also about the place of women in the CID and, as he waited for Sarah in the front hall of the hospital, he smiled to himself at the thought of what Doctor Melrose would have had to say about that had she known. His concerns that they weren't tough enough, either mentally or physically, that their domestic responsibilities in most cases would make the irregular hours impossible, that although being good at what they were told to do, they were not so good at showing initiative, would have been dismissed with scorn. Typical male prejudice, a patronizing attitude, you never give them a chance, absolute nonsense would probably have been the things she would have said, but was that true?

So far, Sarah had been a delight to work with; she had been conscientious, quick on the uptake and yet he still had his doubts. Maskell had his suspicions that she might be mixed up with Painter and wanted him to keep an eye on her. A study of her personal file had shown no lack of intelligence; she had good 'A' levels in English and History, but on the other hand, her upbringing had been remarkably restricted with none of the interesting jobs or trips overseas that many of her contemporaries had achieved. Obviously the fact that she had got stuck with her old father was not her fault and indeed showed loyalty, but surely that was going to interfere with her career.

There was another thing, too; he had been in one of the cubicles in the men's toilet one day when Painter had come in with one of his cronies. The man had a good deal to say about her sexual naïvety and what measures he would like to take to remedy it and at the time he had dismissed it as typical of the bombastic lout's coarse behaviour. However, Donovan had obviously had the same impression as he had himself, although he had to admit that she had handled both Tredgold and the revealing photographs in the presbytery with complete lack of embarrassment. On the plus side, too, she was like a breath of fresh air after the worthy, but plodding Sergeant Bristow, having really shone at the weekend and having achieved more in a couple of days than had that worthy in as many years, but then there had been her stupid behaviour with Pentland.

Tyrrell was extremely sensitive to other people's states of mind and equally adept at hiding his awareness of it from them. He was expecting there to be an awkwardness between them in view of the telling-off he had given her, but there was more to it than that. It wasn't anything that she had said on their walk to the restaurant on the first floor of the pub half a mile up the road, or while they were having lunch, but he was still quite certain that something else had happened to her that morning. She ate very little, which he guessed was most unlike her, and he could see the rapid beat of a pulse in her neck. Should he say anything, or not? Perhaps her personal difficulties would best be left out for the time being, but there could be no putting off the problem of Painter.

'The last thing I want to do is to introduce any unnecessary distractions during this case,' he said, looking straight at her, 'particularly as you have been doing so well. Forget about Pentland, there is something else I need to get out into the open. While it is true that Bert Bristow is out of action and I did need a new assistant, the real reason why Maskell asked me to take you on is that Painter is in it up to his neck. He's been suspended and although at the moment I'm not at liberty to tell you why, I just wanted to warn you that the investigating team are going to question you very thoroughly, very thoroughly indeed. You were with him for nine months or so and they will want to know exactly what duties he gave you to do, what his movements were and what he said to you. Don't try to hide anything out of a misguided sense of loyalty and I'm sure you'll be all right.'

Sarah finished her mouthful of bread and cheese with the greatest of difficulty, hardly being able to swallow, then pushed her plate to one side, glancing up to see Tyrrell looking at her intently.

'Is anything wrong?'

'I already know about Painter and with that Pentland business as well, I think I'm going to have to resign.'

'Whatever for?'

Sarah told him exactly what had happened the previous evening, leaving out nothing. 'I know that it must sound as if I acted calmly and deliberately in not waiting for the squad car to arrive and in wiping off my fingerprints and not giving my name when I made that 999 call, but it wasn't like that at all. I was so shocked that I hardly knew what I was doing, but one thing I did know and that was that I had to protect myself. I'm all mixed up about men and sex as it is and the thought of having to answer questions about how Painter got me to the house, what he did and threatened to do, not to mention the possible pressure to have a physical examination, was too much for me. I acted instinctively, but even if I had had more time to think, I'd have done exactly the same thing again. My life wouldn't be worth living in the force if it all came out; it's just the sort of story that would be meat and drink to the tabloids, let alone the others at work. I know they all think that I'm prudish and a goody-goody and I couldn't face it, I really couldn't.'

'You have no need to worry about Painter. What happened with you and him has nothing to do with his other problems and if you don't wish to press a complaint against him, who's to know about it? It can be strictly between the two of us. You had a horrible experience and coped quite admirably with it and although it's bound to take you time to get over it, it's all in the past now.'

'But what about the man himself? It's just the sort of thing he might embellish and boast about.'

'Painter can't even remember how he got into the house, let alone anything about a mystery woman who made the 999 call and for once I'm inclined to believe him. He was unconscious for a good six hours and the police surgeon said that what they call retrograde amnesia is quite common in a head injury of that severity. Incidentally, you did a good job on his collar bone – broke it as clean as a whistle.'

'I've never hit anyone before – I could have killed him.'

'You did all that was necessary, no more and no less. You also did us a major favour; the man who owns that house was thought to be a respectable Moroccan businessman, but it looks as if he's the big gun behind the drugs' syndicate that Painter was supposed to be investigating. A lot of incriminating documents were found in a safe disguised as a dishwasher in the kitchen and your ex-boss isn't going to wriggle out of this one – he's in it up to his ears. No wonder he never let you do anything when you were working for him, but at least that means that none of the mud will stick to you. As for the Pentland affair, I've said all that is necessary about that, I'm quite sure that you've learned your lesson and as far as I'm concerned that matter is closed. All right? Now, how about another drink?'

'No, thank you.'

'You look all in. Why not take the rest of the week off?'

'No, I'm all right and I couldn't possibly let you and Michael down. I'm not meaning to boast, but I can understand him really well and I'm sure he's on to something; he was quite excited last night.'

Tyrrell smiled. 'All right, you win. Let's forget Painter and get down to what we're in this business for.' He looked down at his notes. 'I had quite an interesting talk with Margaret Melrose this morning. She was a bit abrasive to start with, but after that it went reasonably well. When I got into the hospital, she was already at work in the ITU and—'

'It would seriously disrupt the routine and, in any case, I don't think Doctor Longley would agree to our taking Michael to the chapel again in the middle of the week.'

'I cleared it with him before coming here.'

Margaret Melrose looked up sharply. 'Well, if you've managed to work that miracle and you really think it's necessary, I won't put obstacles in your way. No doubt you've done the same with Mr Calvert.'

'Thanks for reminding me; I'd clean forgotten about him.'

'That man likes to think that he owns the chapel. I was organizing a concert last Christmas to help with the fund-raising and for goodness' sake, only members of the hospital staff were taking part, but he flatly refused to let us use it. Anyone would have thought that I wanted to use it for a strip show; it was nothing more than spite.'

'Spite?'

'We don't get on. We took opposite sides in a debate last year on the question of women bishops in the Church of England. Admittedly, with my dislike of organized religion in any shape or form, I was speaking from a position of some weakness, which he didn't fail to exploit, but I managed to get in a few barbs myself and he lost his temper. The man's highly intelligent and I've never seen him like that before. Perhaps he couldn't bear a woman poking fun at him, particularly as it was so unexpected.'

'Unexpected?'

'Yes. Haven't you heard? I don't possess a sense of humour.'

'I don't believe that.'

'It's true, as a matter of fact. Anyway, it was Father Carey who put me up to it. He told me that it would be a sure way of getting under the man's skin – he even gave me hints about what to say.'

'Such as?'

'He told me that Calvert had a fearsome mother, who

had terrified him all his life and that he had the reverse of an Oedipus complex, which was why he had never married. It wasn't really fair and afterwards, I was ashamed of what I'd said.'

'What about Father Carey? Did he take part in the debate?'

'No, and I remember his exact words, said with a twinkle in his eye. "I've been taught since the cradle that you accept truths, you don't debate them. Anyway, I'm too old now to change and I can't afford to be shown up by young, bright things running intellectual rings around me – it would be bad for my image." As you may have heard, I'm no great respecter of male egos, but one could never get cross with Father Carey for long.'

'So you quite liked him?'

'There were attractive facets to his personality, but I like the concept of Roman Catholic priests and nuns even less than the Anglican variety.'

'What have you against nuns?'

'Everything. They are the product of a male dominated church, which encourages the view that women are basically masochists, who can be shut away in enclosed groups, putting themselves through privations and physical discomfort in the fond hope that they are pleasing God. A God, be it noted, who is an all-powerful male. I find the whole concept nauseating.'

'Monks are surely not that different.'

'Oh, but they are. There are far fewer of them, the majority are drop-outs who can't cope with the world and like most men in enclosed groups, they make a cosy club out of it. That's very different from the women, many of whom, particularly in the country of Father Carey's birth, were forced into it.'

'Do you know any nuns personally?'

'This conversation is getting rather far from the object of your enquiry, isn't it?'

'Perhaps. From what you said earlier, I imagine that Carey and Calvert were at daggers drawn.'

'Not a bit of it. They were like the two men, Campbell and McLeod in Somerset Maugham's story *Sanatorium*, who spent their whole time taking digs at one another. On the surface, it appeared that they hated each other, but when one of them, I think it was McLeod, died, Campbell had nothing left to live for. I'm not saying that Carey and Calvert were quite like that, they seemed to be genuinely good friends, but, nonetheless, they enjoyed taking a rise out of one another whenever the opportunity arose.'

'You've mentioned on a couple of occasions the fact that I might have problems with Doctor Longley; do you find him difficult?'

'I have the greatest respect for Doctor Longley. He was the one at this hospital to have the vision to start an ITU in this place, long before such things were fashionable, and he's an excellent physician as well as being formidable in committee. Despite all the cuts, the facilities and equipment in it are first class and that's largely thanks to him.'

'But he can be difficult?'

'We all have our foibles. But if one is straight with him and works hard, things run pretty smoothly.'

'Is he sexist?'

'Not as far as I'm concerned. He treats me as an honorary male, which I find perfectly satisfactory.'

It was said, Tyrrell thought, without a hint of a smile or a trace of irony and he decided that she meant exactly what she had said.

'What's more,' she continued, 'he's good at delegating

and doesn't interfere with my special interest, which is the control of respiration.'

'As you must have heard by now, Father Carey was poisoned – he left his hip flask on the table behind Michael's bed during that Mass and that's when we think it was tampered with. Were there a lot of people who might have had access to it?'

Margaret Melrose thought for a moment or two. 'Any number. You have to remember that that Mass was a very emotional affair, even for non-believers. It's not often that we have a patient like Michael in the unit for months at a time and most of those looking after him became very upset in their various ways – that's why there was such a big turn-out. Some believe it to be a crime that he has been kept alive when there's no realistic hope now of him improving, others consider that it is merely a technical exercise and try, with varying degrees of success, to shut out all the emotion and finally, there are some who are profoundly disturbed by the tragedy of it. Perhaps the majority have reacted with an element of all three. Carey spent hours talking to him and a cynic might say that what he was really doing was talking to himself, while others no doubt maintain that he was the only one of us all who made any real attempt to meet Michael's emotional needs.'

'I gather that his sermon was pitched pretty strongly.'

'Yes, both strongly and unfairly. Someone delivering a sermon like that is in a privileged position and many people think that what is said on occasions like that can neither be criticized nor questioned.'

'And you don't agree with what he said?'

'Certainly not and I told him so in no uncertain terms afterwards. Clifford Longley and I may disagree on the AIDS question, but at least we are able to discuss it rationally and don't fire off ill-disguised criticisms at each other in public.'

'Are there many people here who disliked Father Carey?'

'I've no idea, but it has occurred to me that someone might have been unwise enough to have confessed something or confided in a man who both drank and liked to gossip, found out that he was releasing juicy bits and then decided to silence him.'

The telephone rang and the anaesthetist reached out and picked up the receiver. 'Right, I will be down shortly.' She got to her feet. 'Some relatives to see. Now, about this visit to the chapel; would late this afternoon suit you, say about five-thirty?'

'I doubt if that would give us long enough to get everyone together.'

'You mean that you want all those who were present at the Mass to go down to the chapel with Michael again?'

'That's right.'

'But there's no hope of achieving that.'

'I don't see why; after all, they were prepared to go there to support Michael before.'

'That was quite different.'

'I agree. On this occasion we are trying to track down a murderer and one could argue that that is even more important.'

For the first time since he had met her, Tyrrell could see that he had got under the anaesthetist's skin. It was obvious that she thought that it was a thoroughly bad idea, but was unable to come up with a reasonable argument against it.

'Well, if you insist, there is nothing I can do about it, but I don't have the time to help you to organize it.'

Tyrrell was expecting much the same reaction from Father Calvert, but was agreeably surprised to find the man in a particularly benign mood.

'Of course you must do it,' he said, 'just name the time. What do you hope to learn?'

'I'm not a great believer in reconstructing crimes, but it sometimes jogs people's memories. I know you weren't there before, but would it be imposing too much on you to ask if you would stand in for Father Carey? I don't mean anything dramatic such as dressing in his robes; it would merely be a question of coming out of the vestry and going up to the altar and then walking back again after an interval.'

'Be glad to if it's going to help to find Patrick's murderer. Life's not going to be the same without him. He used to enjoy needling me and I won't say that it didn't irritate me at times, but life is so much duller now without him and I miss the chess and those meals together. I couldn't stand that Irish biddy, Mrs O'What's-her-name, but she did know how to cook, I have to admit that.'

That particular hurdle over, Tyrrell went back to wait for Longley, who was lecturing to the nurses.

'What's the problem now?' he said, when he caught sight of the detective when he left the amphitheatre.

'Without naming any names, I've been meeting with a certain reluctance of some people to co-operate with Michael's visit to the chapel.'

'That fellow Calvert, I suppose.'

'No, he was very helpful.'

'You surprise me. Who was it, then? Never mind, I'll do some stirring for you.' He strode into his office and picked up the phone. 'Doctor Longley here, would you ask Doctor Lee to come to my room on the second floor at once please?' He replaced the receiver and without offering any explanation, started to write on the pad in front of him. 'Ah, there you are,' he said when the young woman in the white coat was shown in by his secretary. 'I would like you to tell all the people on this list to be in the chapel at six o'clock tomorrow evening – that suit you, Tyrrell?'

'Admirably.'

'And should they show any reluctance, perhaps you'd ask them to explain themselves to me in person. Are you familiar with the expression "obstructing the police in the course of their enquiries"?'

'Yes, sir.'

'Use it, if necessary. Pentland will be responsible for seeing that Donovan gets down there and back safely. Is that quite clear?'

'Yes, sir.'

'Good. See to it right away, would you please?' The physician waited until the young woman had gone. 'I like female SHOs; they're very good at doing what they're told.'

'I imagine that they are.'

'And so you see, thanks largely to Clifford Longley, Michael's visit to the chapel has been fixed for tomorrow at six,' Tyrrell said. 'The more I see of that man, the more interesting do I find him. By and large the males, Boyd, Carey and Michael, for example, don't and didn't like him, whereas the women seem to eat out of his hand, even Margaret Melrose. They have a way of looking at him with doe eyes – you should have seen that SHO of his, Doctor Lee. He's certainly got more than a healthy bank balance and do you suppose that he brought his deadly charm to bear on Claire Garrard and was that why she tried to get

Pentland to beat the Devil out of her? I think that another word with her, perhaps tomorrow morning, directly she comes off duty, would be in order.'

'Do you think she might have confessed something to Father Carey?'

'It had crossed my mind. See what you can discover this afternoon about that community of hers, would you? It might give us an idea about the best line to take with her. Now, what about the others? Pentland certainly did confide in Carey, but did he do more than confiding when he went round to the presbytery? In a muddle about sex, disastrous experience with Claire Garrard, too much to drink – stranger things have happened. Margaret Melrose and Longley were also at the mass. She's a very tough and cool customer indeed and clearly didn't want to go down to the chapel again with Michael and when I asked her about nuns, she made it only too clear that she held no brief for them at all. Does that mean that she knows about Claire Garrard? As for Longley, although he didn't like Carey one bit, he was quite open about it and disliking someone is hardly an adequate motive for killing them.'

'We'll just have to hope that Michael comes up with something tomorrow.'

'And so say all of us.'

CHAPTER ELEVEN

By the time she had been to several libraries and tried to find the Community of the Suffering of Christ and failed to find a single reference to it in either location, Sarah was not only feeling frustrated, but also anxious; if she was to fail something as simple as that, how was she going to convince Tyrrell that she was up to the task of continuing to work on the case, particularly when it was only too clear that he had reservations about her? It wasn't only that; every time she tried to concentrate on the problem, the memory of that scene with Arthur Prescott – she had already stopped thinking about him as her father – kept blotting everything else out, and she wasn't able to get Painter out of her mind, either.

She desperately needed to talk to someone about it and the obvious person was her Uncle Henry. Surely, though, he must have known about it all along and if he did, why hadn't he told her about it years ago? Perhaps if she were to ask him about religious communities – he always seemed to have knowledge of that sort of thing at his fingertips and if he didn't, knew someone who did – she might be able to introduce the subject of Arthur Prescott suddenly and catch him unawares.

Back at the Yard, she gave her uncle a ring on the

number he had given her to use in an emergency, which she had been told to memorize and never write down. Sarah had never been quite sure whether he meant that seriously, or if he was playing one of his dry jokes on her. At times, during some of her wilder speculations about what he did, she told herself that she had been reading too many spy stories, but at others, she didn't quite believe that he merely had a boring routine job in the Civil Service – he seemed to be able to pull too many strings for that. She had often wondered, too, if his influence had played a part in her getting into the CID.

'Hello, young Sarah,' he said. 'Good to hear from you; I've been wondering how you were getting on.'

'Pretty well, thanks. I've got a new job with one of the chief inspectors and at long last I've been given things to do on my own. I'm involved in a murder case at the moment and I'm trying to find out something about a convent in Northumberland called the Community of the Suffering of Christ.'

'Good grief! Not thinking of taking the veil, I trust.'

'It's true that I'm trying to lose some weight, but I'm not that desperate – yet.'

His chuckle came clearly over the line. 'For one moment you had me anticipating the look on your father's face when he heard the news. By the way, how is my pet aversion?'

'Much the same as usual.'

'You surprise me! When do you need this information by?'

'Tomorrow morning, I'm afraid.'

'What exactly do you want to know?'

'What goes on in a place like that; what happens to people who can't take it and come out; what effects it might have on those who have the wrong type of personality for that type of life.'

'Hmm. I'll see what I can do. I'll ring you back in half an hour.'

He had rung off before she could ask if she could see him – the telephone was absolutely hopeless for the long discussion she needed to have with him – and she was still wondering how to put it to him, when precisely at the time he had said, he came back on the line.

'There's a fellow I know a bit who's an expert on cults, religious and otherwise, brain washing and terrorism. He's invited you out to dinner at the Athenaeum tonight.'

'The Athenaeum? Do they allow women in?'

'My dear Sarah, where have you been? Women are all powerful these days – hardly any previously secure male sanctum is proof against them. I wish I could meet you there for dinner, but unfortunately I have to work late this evening. With any luck, though, I should be able to join you for coffee and a brandy.'

'Do you think you could? There is something even more important I need to discuss with you.'

'Yes, of course. Anyway, it will give me just the excuse I've been looking for to leave work at a reasonable hour. Oh, by the way, don't be put off by Hugo Lindsay's appearance; he looks like a mildly demented and avuncular bishop, but in fact he's as sharp as a needle and Professor of Forensic Psychiatry at St Gregory's Hospital. You're expected at eight. Don't be late.'

Sarah was disappointed in neither the dinner, which was excellent, nor in Professor Lindsay. He was a massive teddy bear of a man with a rubicund face, who had the habit of resting his hands on his very considerable paunch and beaming at everyone around him. Sarah didn't think she had ever seen anyone eat and drink quite so much in one sitting, or with such relish. Whitebait, an enormous steak with two helpings of vegetables, was followed by apple pie and cream, with a liberal quantity of Stilton to finish.

'Business never did mix with a good meal,' he said contemplating with pleasure his second large brandy, which was set to follow most of the bottle of burgundy he had consumed with his meal. 'Now, what can I do for you?'

'I think that a woman in her late twenties may have poisoned someone. She is the elder daughter of a retired army officer and was sent to a convent boarding-school, although she was a non-Catholic. Largely, I suspect, to get away from him, she became a convert and joined the Community of the Suffering of Christ in Northumberland. I don't know whether she became a fully-fledged nun or not, but she is now a nursing sister on night duty at a London teaching hospital. She has masochistic tendencies and possesses a small whip made of knotted cords. The murdered man was a Catholic priest. Oh yes, one other thing, her sister, who was taken away from the same school by her father, died recently from an overdose of drugs, possibly accidental. I'd be very interested to hear your reactions to all that and if you are able to give me any information about that order.'

'I wish my junior staff were half as good at summing up cases as you are, my dear; it would save an awful lot of time and unnecessary verbiage. Now, let me see. I have made something of a study of cults and religious orders and I am familiar with the order in which you have expressed an interest. It is something of an anachronism, sticking to the old idea of aiming to break down the will and judgement of the individual so that they accept the will of God and of whoever else wishes to impose it on them.'

'Brainwashing, in fact.'

'Exactly. The trouble these days with orders like that is that they are rooted in the Victorian view of women and they have not advanced beyond that. The origin of the full-length black habit is from that period and it even survived Pope John 23rd and the Second Vatican Council. The novices have a very hard time; for two years they are isolated from the world; they read no books other than spiritual ones and they must subject themselves to constant self-examination. They also believe in corporal mortification, eating what they dislike, getting up the very instant they are called and they are encouraged to use a "discipline", which your night sister obviously retained, on themselves. If used across the shoulders it is known as "superior discipline" and I leave the "inferior variety" to your imagination.'

'They don't still do that, do they?'

'Indeed they do and various other humiliating acts, such as kissing the feet of all the nuns in the refectory during special penances.'

'I find that absolutely horrifying; how could anyone do that?'

'Very easily is the answer. It doesn't only happen in the religious life, you know, but in the secular as well. Armies, totalitarian states and' – he gave a little bow – 'even the police in some parts of the world treat their trainees every bit as harshly and often the victims come to believe that they deserve the things that are done to them and that the acts they are ordered to undertake later on, however brutal they may be, are justified and even right. How else do you get people to burn heretics and, in our day, torture political prisoners?'

'How do people manage to get out of an order like the one I'm interested in?'

'That's not difficult to start with; in fact, many fail to make the grade. There is a long probationary period, first as a postulant and then as a novitiate and during that two and a half years or so, quite a few fall out. Once, though, anyone becomes a professed nun, they are allowed to have contact with the secular world and may train to become doctors, nurses and teachers. It is not a contemplative order. At that stage and afterwards, it requires a good deal of courage to leave. The world has moved on, families have often broken up and there is the terrible guilt engendered by failure.'

'What about sex?'

'The aim is to sublimate it completely, which is why they discourage what they somewhat coyly describe as "particular friendships". It works for some, but there are endless problems for those for whom it doesn't.'

'And what about those who do leave later on?'

'Not many do, which is why it is so difficult to generalize. I would guess that it would depend on why the person went into the order in the first place. As for sex, some no doubt are just not worried by impulses in that direction at all and happily remain celibate, while others are the very reverse. It's the latter group that has the potential to get torn apart by it.'

'How might one of those react to being seduced?'

'Did that happen to your subject?'

'I think it quite likely.'

'It would depend on who did the seducing and how it was carried out.'

'My guess would be an older man and one who is a real expert.'

'Without knowing your subject or the man in question, that is an impossible question to answer. On the one hand, if he did it skilfully and she enjoyed it, it might just possibly unlock her inhibitions, but on the other, the very pleasure might produce intolerable feelings of guilt. If the experience was distasteful, or worse, it might well put her off for good. Not very helpful, I'm afraid.'

'Oh, but it is, very. Can you see someone like the person I have described having the impulse to kill?'

'The Catholic priest?'

'Yes.'

'It depends on why she left the order, on her personality and if she had reason enough to hate him, or want to silence him. How was the murder done?'

'With an extract of *amanita phalloides* put into the whiskey in his hip flask.'

'Hmm. Traditionally, poison is a woman's weapon, but that isn't by any means always the case. The murder was obviously premeditated, though.'

'Yes, it most certainly was. The ex-nun did try to get herself beaten with her "discipline" by one of the junior doctors not long before the murder; he didn't do so and fled from the scene, but he was so upset by what had happened – he is also a Catholic and very mixed up about sex – that he talked to the priest about it and it seems very likely that she found out that he had.'

'You're pretty certain that she did it, aren't you?'

'She is the most obvious suspect, but I mustn't jump to premature conclusions. I haven't spoken to her yet and still haven't quite got the feel of her order.'

The psychiatrist talked for the best part of an hour and

Sarah found it totally absorbing. He told her about Ignation obedience, the methods used to break down the will and the critical faculties, the penances required and the mortifications practised.

'The term "nun" was originally applied to women who went into totally enclosed orders; they remained in convents all their lives, which they dedicated to prayer and contemplation. It was St Vincent de Paul who founded an order of a different kind, which allowed the women to go out to work amongst the poor and they became known as Sisters of Charity, something the hierarchy didn't like at all at the time.'

'And the Community of the Suffering of Christ is one of those?'

'That's right and it's ironic that nowadays they are considered by the Church to be too strict. In that particular order, the nuns have a tradition of working in the medical field, both as doctors and nurses, and that training period is desperately hard as well. There is none of the camaraderie that keeps the usual run of students going with the sharing of experiences and the friendships that develop. For them, it is just a constant grind. It means getting up very early in the morning so that by nine o'clock there has already been three and a half hours of prayer, Mass and manual work – no wonder they get exhausted.'

'So they're not allowed to live away from their communities.'

'No. The hold on them remains extremely tight.'

Sarah shook her head. 'I don't see how anyone can put up with a life like that.'

'I wouldn't want to give the impression that any more than a small minority are anything but serene, fulfilled and totally dedicated. I have met several and they have been truly happy, but it does require a true vocation and the right personality.'

'I still don't understand.'

'That's because you look at it from your own perspective. To understand properly you have to have been through it or something similar yourself.'

'But I imagine that if you turn against it, feelings against the system may be equally strong.'

'Most certainly. That can follow disillusionment with any form of conversion, sacred or profane.'

Lindsay suddenly started to get to his feet and, as the armchair was a deep one, it was an exercise that took a great deal of effort.

'Excuse me, my dear, but I just caught sight of your uncle through the door and he looked distinctly lost. Would you excuse me if I left you now? I promised my wife that I wouldn't be late home.'

'Of course. Thank you so much for the delicious dinner and for all the fascinating information. I'm tremendously grateful.'

He shook her gravely by the hand. 'The pleasure was entirely mine.'

Sarah watched him lumber out of the room, wondering for a moment if she had been foolish not to have given in to the impulse to tell him about what had happened to her with Painter and then decided that she hadn't. She went across to the massive mahogany round table and leafed through a copy of *Country Life* until her uncle walked in briskly and kissed her on the cheek.

'You've made a conquest, Sarah, my dear. Lindsay was most impressed; he seems to think that you're wasted in the CID and that you ought to take up medicine. Did you find out what you wanted to know?'

'Yes, thank you. He was really excellent, but I do feel guilty about having taken up the whole of his evening.'

'You did him a favour. Don't tell anyone else, but the eminent professor is nagged and bullied unmercifully by his wife. The fellow should never have got married – he's not the type.'

'The same as you, Uncle Henry?'

Her uncle wasn't in the least put out. 'Not exactly the same,' he said, patting his trim waistline, 'but I must confess that in other ways there are similarities. Ah, here comes my brandy.' He took the glass off the silver salver and nodded his thanks to the elderly, uniformed club servant. 'Anything for you, Sarah?'

'No, thank you, except perhaps for another coffee.'

'Two black coffees then, Parker, if you please.'

'Very good, Sir Henry.'

Her uncle looked at her over the top of his brandy glass with his deceptively soft brown eyes.

'Something important's happened, hasn't it?'

'How did you know?'

'I've spent the last thirty years having to sum people up quickly and I suppose that noticing subtle changes in them has become instinctive.'

'Yes, you're right, something certainly has happened.' Sarah looked round as the tall, thin man, whose clerical collar was fighting a losing battle with his prominent Adam's apple, and who had sat down next to them and begun to sip his coffee noisily. 'Is there anywhere quiet we could go?'

'Yes, of course. How about the small library? No one will disturb us up there.'

Sarah had been so absorbed by what Professor Lindsay had been telling her after dinner that the events of both the previous evening and of that morning had lost some of their impact. But now it all came flooding back. She could feel the tears threatening to break loose and looked determinedly at the rows of leather-bound books on the shelves against the wall opposite her.

'When you supported my idea of joining the police, I jumped at the chance, not because I knew what I was letting myself in for, but because my father didn't want me to do it. In a way, I suppose you could say that it was my first act of rebellion, even if it was a pretty feeble one. I enjoyed the training, and meeting all sorts of people certainly made me grow up, but over the last year, ever since joining the CID, I became convinced that I had made a terrible mistake. I hated the man I was working for, the jobs he gave me to do were boring and I very nearly handed in my resignation. In fact, the only things that enabled me to keep going were that I didn't want to let you down and I couldn't have borne Father's inevitable "I told you so" attitude. All that changed a week ago. As I told you on the phone, I've been given a really good chance to prove to myself that I'm up to it and the new job is everything I could have asked for. I respect the man I'm now working for, the case is both interesting and challenging and I absolutely love it. It does mean, though, working for long and unpredictable hours like this evening and—'

'And the snag is your father?'

Sarah nodded. 'When even he could see that it wouldn't be possible for me to spend my whole time being his housekeeper, he decided that the best job for me would be as a secretary in his old firm of accountants and so he paid for me to do a shorthand and word-processing course. He was violently opposed to my going into the police force, but when he found that it didn't seriously interfere with his own life, he accepted it. In the last week, though, during which he has been having to get some of his own meals, we have hardly been speaking and this morning I took the plunge and told him that I was going to leave and get a place of my own after finding him a living-in house-keeper.'

'Good for you. What was his reaction?'

'He told me that he wasn't my father and that he only married Mum because— Oh, Uncle Henry, why didn't you tell me?'

'Oh Sarah, my dear.'

His tone of voice and the hug he gave her was just too much for her control and she cried as she had never cried in her life before. She was crying for the mother she had lost, for the years of looking after the selfish old man, whom she had tried so hard not to hate, because she still hadn't got over her experience with Painter and with relief at long last being able to give way.

Her uncle didn't say anything then, just rocked her gently until she had calmed down.

'The reason I didn't tell you, Sarah, my dear, was that I didn't know. I can't think why I was so blind – it explains everything. After your experience with Arthur, you no doubt believe that life can be very unfair to women now and you would be right, but in the thirty or so years after the war, it was a great deal worse. When our parents died within a year or two of each other, Margaret, who had never left home, was nearly forty, she had had no training of any sort and precious little money. Father had put most of his savings into some hare-brained scheme and lost practically the lot, the house was heavily mortgaged and I was unable to help, only just having left university and starting in the Civil Service. To her great credit, she buckled to, like you, did a secretarial course and found a job in Arthur's firm.

'I was happy for her when she got married, although I could have wished that she hadn't done so secretly without telling me. The reason for that became clear when you were born and I realized that they had adjusted the date of their wedding to make it respectable. It was obvious to me that Margaret must have been forced into it; why else, I thought, had she chosen someone as old and arid as Arthur? At first, I was so angry that I could hardly bear to be civil to him – I was certain that Margaret had been sexually inexperienced and probably ignorant as well, and to use an old-fashioned phrase, thought that he had taken advantage of her – but then I saw how happy she was with you and believed that it might turn out well after all.

'You were such a lively and friendly child that I found it difficult to believe that Arthur could have played any part in your creation, but now it sticks out a mile that my instinct was correct. Why did I put such thoughts to one side? I suppose it was because I had no wish to interfere in someone else's life and partly also that Margaret never gave the slightest hint about it, not even when she was dying. I did worry about your future, but she made me promise not to stick my oar in. "I know you don't like Arthur", she said to me, when I saw her in hospital when she was having her last course of radiotherapy, "but he has been very good to me and Sarah. You will be nice to him, won't you?"

'Naturally I agreed and when she assured me that he had always taken an interest in your future and believed in education for women, I was to some extent reassured.

That didn't last long, though, and after that time when he hit you, I was determined that you weren't going to get trapped by him. I was so pleased when you chose the police force. I knew quite a bit about it, that there were fine career prospects for women and I remembered how national service had given me the education about life that you had missed out on. All right, so I exerted a little influence to get you an interview, but you've been on your own ever since and I can see that everything's beginning to come together.'

'So you don't know who my real father was?'

Garnett shook his head. 'No I don't and I think it very likely that it would be impossible for you to find out. As you may know, under the Children Act of 1975, adopted people, that is those over the age of eighteen, may apply to the Registrar General for information which will lead them to the original record of their birth, provided that they have been counselled first, but in your case, my guess would be that Arthur, with your mother's agreement, probably claimed to be your real father. If that was accepted, and I can think of no reason why it shouldn't have been, then there is no further avenue open to you. Just be thankful that whoever your father was, he and your mother have provided you with courage, energy and intelligence, not to mention good looks.'

'It's a funny thing, but all I could think of this morning after Arthur told me was relief that he wasn't my father – he is such a selfish man – but he must be very lonely and I can see why he resented me and, in his own way, he must have loved Mum.'

'He had no reason to resent you and if you're thinking that you owe him anything, you've repaid any debt a hundredfold over the last ten years. Now, don't let us forget the practicalities.' He pulled a slim, leather-bound diary out of the breast pocket of his jacket and leafed through the pages. 'My advice to you is to forget about Arthur and concentrate on this case of yours; as you said yourself, this is your big chance to make an impression and you don't want to let it slip. Come back to Fulham with me now, pack a bag and then you can stay in my flat until the case is over and you have the opportunity to find a place of your own.'

'But what about Fath— Arthur?'

'Leave Arthur to me. I would enjoy a chat with him after all this time.' He laughed. 'Don't worry, I'm not going to beat him up, or even tell him a few home truths. I'll have to make some arrangements for him and either he can stay in my house in Sussex until my secretary finds him a housekeeper, or, if he prefers he can go into a hotel, or even fend for himself.'

CHAPTER TWELVE

Claire Garrard closed the door of her flat carefully behind her, took off her cap, uniform and tights, put on her dressing-gown and then went into the kitchenette to make herself a cup of tea. Her hip was hurting abominably, but constant pain had been her companion for so long that it had become part of her, almost like the chain with tiny spikes on it that she had worn around the top of her arm when she had been a postulant. She let out a weary sigh when she heard the soft tap at the door. There were advantages in having Valerie Fletcher in the adjoining flat – she didn't play loud music or hold parties in there – but there were snags, too: she was forever running out of something and coming to borrow milk, sugar, or the iron.

'I know that you must be wanting to get to bed, but we were wondering if we might have a quick word with you.'

Claire Garrard was so used to suppressing her emotions that her expression didn't alter when she saw the two detectives standing at the door, her gaze merely dropping as it always did when she was faced by people in authority.

'Come in. May I get you a cup of tea?'

'Thank you, we'd enjoy that, if you're sure it's not too much trouble.'

The brief respite as she went into the kitchen only served to heighten the anxiety she had felt directly she had seen them. What had Richard Pentland been saying about her? When she got back, Claire Garrard continued to keep her eyes down, but even so was aware that the tall quietly-spoken man on the other side of the table was looking at her intently.

'Father Carey was murdered by poison, which was put into his hip flask during the Mass he was saying for Michael Donovan. He had put the flask on the table behind Michael's bed and we are sure that that was when it was done. We are trying to build up a picture of where everyone was standing or sitting during the Mass and we would be most grateful for your help.'

Claire Garrard felt the blood draining out of her face. 'Murdered? Are you sure?'

'Yes. I'm sorry it's been such a shock, but I thought that everyone here would have known by now.'

'People don't talk to me much.' She suddenly looked up. 'I may not have liked Father Carey, but I didn't kill him.'

'Why didn't you like him?'

'Because he was a hypocrite and not fit to be a priest. There is a strict rule of celibacy for the Catholic priesthood and Patrick Carey was an active homosexual.'

'That's very interesting. How did you know that?'

'It was common knowledge.'

'And you believed it?'

'Yes. Why else do you suppose that he took up the AIDS cause so strongly?'

'I gather that that was the theme of his sermon.'

'Yes, it was and he was using his privileged position to attack me and Doctor Longley.'

'You don't approve of having AIDS patients at St Cuthbert's then?'

'No. Obviously they have to be looked after well, but in units that are geared to cope with them. Having them scattered in many different places creates tensions, risks to the staff and leads to poor care. It wasn't fair that people like me and Doctor Longley should have been pilloried for speaking out for what we believe to be right for the hospital.'

'Do you disapprove of homosexuals?'

'Disapprove is not the right word; I believe that they offend against God and that they are to be pitied.'

'The Catholic Church must put great strain on those people with strong sex drives.'

'There is always the sacrament of marriage.'

'Very true, but I was thinking about priests and nuns. If people are cloistered together for long periods of time with only those of their own sex, it must surely present grave problems with those who are unable to sublimate their desires.'

'You know about me, don't you?'

'That you were a nun?'

'Yes.'

'Who told you?'

'We are trained to observe things; you almost always keep your gaze averted from people's faces, you sit unnaturally still, and I couldn't help but notice the calluses on your knees when you sat down just now. You must have found it very hard to adjust to life outside your order.'

'It was and although I left several years ago, I still haven't done so and I doubt if I ever will. I realize now that I only joined to escape the tyranny of my father, but all I succeeded in doing was to find another – I never had a true vocation, whatever I may have thought at the time. I left the order because I could no longer bear the pettiness of all the regulations, the detachment from the real world and the subordination of all my individuality to the system. I have no doubt at all that my father got pleasure out of ridiculing me because of my hip, humiliating and punishing me, but what upset me more than anything were the feelings of guilt at the realization that I got pleasure out of that sort of thing.'

'After having been in a religious order for so many years it must also have been very difficult for you to make friends when you came out.'

'It was and had it not been for Doctor Longley, I don't think I would have been able to get through the last few weeks.'

'What has been particularly bad about the last few weeks?'

'My sister died from a drugs' overdose recently – it wasn't suicide, she was an addict and was so damaged that she completely lost control of what she was taking. I appealed to Doctor Longley to admit her to the ITU here, knowing how good it is, and he not only did so, but kept the secret that she was my sister – I took a different name when I left the order. He was a great comfort to me in all sorts of ways, particularly after she died. I was under great strain and as a result was fool enough to have a row with Father Carey after he had accused me of not caring for Michael. All I did was forget to pass on a message and I had so many other things on my mind. When I first came here, I trusted that man; I talked to him and went to him as a confessor, but then I saw how much he drank, I heard the gossip about him and then lost all confidence in him. Worse, I thought he had been dropping hints about me to the others – he was always around the hospital chatting to people and drinking in the bar with the doctors and students.'

'Can't you get away from here for a time?'

'Where would I go? Now that Anna is dead, I have no contacts at all with my family and the order would never allow me to go to one of their retreats.'

'Have you thought of trying one run by a different order? I understand that many of them take lay people nowadays.'

Claire Garrard nodded. 'Perhaps I should. We had to do manual work in the house where I had to live during my nursing training and I found some peace there. There was a mushroom farm attached to it and although some of the others found it boring, I never did.'

'Does anyone here know that you did that type of work?'

'What? On the mushroom farm?'

Tyrrell nodded.

'No.'

'Not even Father Carey?'

'I may have told him. I can't remember.'

Anyone else, Tyrrell thought, would have asked him why he was interested in such a mundane piece of information, but he imagined that if someone had spent a good proportion of their life suppressing questions, it became part of them. He also sensed that although initially she had been worried by their presence, she now didn't want them to depart. As for him, though, he was finding the atmosphere becoming progressively more uncomfortable and it was a considerable relief when he was eventually able to bring the interview to a close.

'What a sad story!' he said to Sarah when they were back in the car.

'Do you believe her?'

'It all fits in with what you discovered about her family, her school and that order. She also had a motive for killing Father Carey, but would she have come out with the fact that she had worked on a mushroom farm if she had done so? I very much doubt it.'

'I suppose it's possible that she wants us to find out and couldn't bring herself to confess directly.'

Tyrrell nodded. 'That's a good point; she's certainly a very disturbed young woman and I must admit that I haven't the slightest idea how someone like that thinks.'

'Why do you suppose that Longley lied to you about knowing her?'

'I don't find that so surprising now that she's told us about her sister. Longley is very much one of the old school and I have no doubt that he would be punctilious about clinical confidences. I've no doubt, though, that at some stage they discussed Father Carey's sermon together – the two of them used very much the same words to describe it.'

Although Sarah wasn't expecting the reconstruction in the chapel to yield anything useful, she didn't like to say so to Roger Tyrrell, let alone Michael Donovan, who clearly didn't share her reservations. She had found that the more she had communicated with the man, the more readily was she able to divine his moods. As soon as he had been placed carefully in the same position as before, she had no doubt that he was excited. The messages from his eyelids were flashing out so quickly that despite her rapidly increasing expertise, she was scarcely able to keep up with him.

'Don't let anyone you know guess about the Morse, or overhear you speaking to me, will you?'

'No, I'll be most careful. Is the mirror set correctly?'

'Yes, but I think the bed is too far forward. Would you move it back a few inches?'

'That better?'

'Yes, I was just able to see the top of the candles before and I can again now. Who's standing in for Father Carey?'

'Father Calvert. He's the resident Anglican chaplain, who likes to be addressed like that. He and Father Carey were good friends and used to play chess together.'

'He wasn't at the Mass, was he?'

'No. He told us that that would be carrying ecumenism too far.'

'I'd like him to go into the vestry and then come out and stand in front of the altar, Once he's there, would you get Longley, Melrose, Pentland, Garrard, Jacquie and Liz in that order to walk behind my bed, stay there for a few moments and then walk away again. Perhaps you'd also watch their reactions as they do so.'

Sarah passed the instructions on to Roger Tyrrell as quietly and discreetly as possible, holding her handkerchief to her lips, which both hid them from those sitting nearby and helped to deaden her voice.

Tyrrell got them all to go through that exercise, then asked Sister Mountfield to try to remember in as much detail as she could where everyone had been positioned close to the bed throughout the Mass and then went back to Michael's side.

'Anything else you'd like me to do?' he whispered.

'Would you ask Sarah to go into the vestry when everyone has gone and then describe it to me as accurately as possible tomorrow night? I've got some more thinking to do and I'm rather tired just now.'

'Of course.'

*

Sarah was surprised to find that Michael had been moved when she went up to the ITU the following evening. He was in a room along the corridor and separate from the ITU and apart from the elaborate-looking bed and the respirator, it contained a bench on one side, on which were several pieces of equipment. The wall immediately to the left of the bed was taken up by a large window, through which she could see what looked like a laboratory, and a communicating door.

'What's this in aid of?' she asked.

'It's the sleep-study and EEG-telemetry room.'

'EEG? That's for measuring brain waves in epilepsy, isn't it?'

'That and other conditions – the letters stand for electroencephalogram. In sleep studies, they do all-night recordings of the patient on video and superimpose the EEG tracing on it. That allows them to correlate the visual appearance of the patient with the electrical findings.'

'But why have they moved you in here?'

'There's a bit of a panic on. They've had to admit some meningitis cases and they've decided to put them together in the ITU where I was before.'

'Isn't it a bit lonely in here?'

'No, I like it. There's a very nice registrar in charge of the set-up and he's told me how it all works and even showed me some recordings on the monitor on the wall-mounting up there. During the recordings it can also be switched through to the nursing station, which is how they keep an eye on the patients in case they have a fit, and now it also enables them to keep tabs on me. So, we'll have to watch our step, won't we?'

Sarah looked up, seeing for the first time the camera hanging from a long arm attached to a bracket in the ceiling.

'We most certainly will.'

'There's a monitor at the nursing station so that the person on duty can see me whenever they want to and there are alarms on the ventilator and cardiac monitors to alert them if anything goes wrong. Doctor Leyland explained all that as well.'

'What happens if there's a power cut?'

'Emergency generators cut in and supply the power. It's a bit tedious for them to have to go out into the corridor to reach me, but it's only a few yards away. The communicating door to the lab is kept locked as is the one that gives access to it from the corridor; Doctor Leyland told me that equipment has gone walkabout in the past and he keeps the keys to them himself.'

'How about lights at night?'

'There's a dimmer switch.'

'And what's this fancy bed?'

'Something new that they're trying out and I'm the guinea pig. It's only on appro, but I think they should buy it. It's great – really comfortable. Warm air is blown through myriads of tiny plastic balls and with the constant, but very slight movement the whole time, I don't have to be turned. I gather, though, it's hellish expensive and very heavy.'

'And what are those things attached to your temples?'

'Just some electrodes that Doctor Leyland has put on. They're attached to that junction box over there on the bench and he's able to make recordings in his laboratory in the basement. He's anxious to know how much interference there is from this bed. They don't bother me and he's been so nice that I was glad to be able to help him out with his experiment.'

'All mod cons!'

'That's right. Were you able to take a look at the vestry?'

'Yes. I asked Father Calvert if I could see Father Carey's robes and he took me in. It's quite small, but there is a large built-in cupboard there, in which vestments, candles and things like that are kept. There's also a safe for the chalice and other valuables. Can you believe it? There was a robbery a few years ago and the collection was stolen, hence the security. There's a single chair in there and, let's see....' She consulted her notebook. 'Ah, yes, there's a mirror set into the other door. Calvert told me that it hadn't been opened for years; evidently at one time there was another corridor on that side leading to the vestry, but the end of it was blocked off to make a large storage space for cleaning equipment.'

'Is the door from the corridor to it kept locked?'

'No. I had a look at it and there are just a few buckets, mops, brushes and a polisher in it.'

'Any windows in the vestry?'

'None at all. Did you get any ideas from that reconstruction in the chapel?'

'One or two. Perhaps we could discuss it again when I've had a chance to put them together?'

'When would you like me to come?'

'Any time tomorrow.'

'All right, you're the boss.'

'You did it, didn't you?'

'Did what?'

'Something about your father.'

'Yes. How did you know?'

'There's an excitement about you. You seem a bit

anxious, but underneath, you're bubbling – I can hear it in your voice – and you've also grown up. A few days ago you would have blushed when I made that remark about TV and now you're able to take that sort of thing in your stride. Tell me about it.'

Sarah did so, not only about her confrontation with her father, but also her experience with Painter.

'That little lot's enough to make anyone grow up. Are you sure you're all right?'

'Yes, I'm fine, I really am. I feel happier and more relaxed than I ever have done before. Tyrrell and my uncle have been a great help, but most of it I owe to you.'

'I haven't done anything.'

'Oh, but you have. If it hadn't been for you, I would never have followed Claire Garrard, I wouldn't have had the confidence to deal with Painter, nor would I have tackled Arthur. I'll always be grateful to you.'

'But where are you going to live now?'

'My uncle has offered to put me up while I look around for a place of my own and what a relief that will be after years of having to keep everything in its proper place, never being able to have friends in and never being able to make the slightest noise. It'll be heaven.'

'That I can well imagine.'

'And most of it really is thanks to you.' She bent over to give him a kiss, not the merest touch this time, but a proper one. 'Goodbye, Michael, see you tomorrow.'

'Are you quite sure you know what to do, nurse?'

'Yes, sister.'

If the woman had asked her that once, Felicity Bryant thought, she had done so half-a-dozen times. What if she was employed by an agency? Surely Sister Garrard must know that she had been trained in Sydney and was experienced in intensive care and it wasn't even as if she had just started this particular job, let alone that it wasn't in the least complicated. What could be easier than looking after a single patient on a ventilator, even if he was tucked away in a room along the corridor from the nursing station, watch a few monitors and answer the phone?

When she had first started the job, a quick look through the notes had shown that there had been no problems with the control of Michael's respiration for weeks and with him being in the new bed, he didn't even have to be turned during the night, not that that would have proved much of a task, she thought, after she had visited him for the third time. The man was lying there motionless with his eyes closed and the matchstick arms stretched out above the single sheet and thin blanket covering the rest of him, he looked so frail that she reckoned she would have been able to lift him quite easily on her own.

On leaving the sleep-study room, she let out a sigh of resignation when she came round the corner in the corridor to see the now familiar figure of Sister Garrard standing at the nursing station.

'Is Michael all right, Nurse Bryant?'

Felicity let out another sigh. Why couldn't the wretched woman leave her alone.

'Yes, Sister, he's sleeping peacefully.'

'Any phone calls since I last came round?'

'No, Sister.'

When the woman had limped her way out of sight, Felicity made a note about her visit to Michael's room and after checking the monitors, settled down to write a long overdue letter to Rob. At least that was her intention, but ten minutes later she still hadn't started it, biting the end of her ball-point pen and staring at the blank airmail letter card. The problem was, that in her case, absence hadn't made the heart grow fonder, which certainly wasn't true as far as he was concerned; he had telephoned as soon as she had arrived in England to stay with her cousin, and letters had appeared in a steady stream thereafter. How was she going to be able to let him down gently?

She was day-dreaming, remembering the good and not so good times they had had together, when the insistent buzzing from the TV monitor jerked her back into reality. On the screen, she could see that Michael was awake and blinking and at the same moment, she heard the sound of the alarm on the ventilator, then she saw the straight line at the bottom of the picture showing that it had stopped.

For a moment or two she sat there almost paralysed by the shock, then pausing only to hit the cardiac-arrest button, she sprinted along the corridor, hardly noticing that the door to the sleep-study room was shut and pressed down the handle. The pain in her right wrist which had taken the full weight of her body as she was brought to a sudden halt and the realization that the door was locked, came through to her simultaneously. It just wasn't possible, she thought; it must be a nightmare. She hit the door with her shoulder, but that hardly even caused it to rattle, merely bruising her, and the kicks she gave it with the sole of her shoe were equally ineffective. It was at that moment that the alarm on the cardiac monitor also went off inside the room and looking round, she caught sight of the fire extinguisher at the end of the corridor. She had just started to attack the door with it when the cardiac-arrest team came running along the passage with their trolley and within seconds the door had given way under the combined assault of the three of them. The anaesthetist and his assistant rushed to the bed and used all the tricks of cardiac resuscitation and manual ventilation, but it was all to no avail.

Felicity Bryant had seen death many times before, but never under any circumstances like this and when the anaesthetist straightened up, shaking his head, she suddenly felt sick and faint. She turned away, only to meet the reproachful gaze of Sister Garrard, who was standing watching the scene through the shattered door.

The phone by Roger Tyrrell's bed rang and, as always under these circumstances, he was awake on the instant and noted the time of 2.35 on the radio alarm clock as he lifted the receiver.

'Tyrrell here.' He listened without comment until the voice at the other end of the line had finished speaking. 'Very well, I'll be there within half an hour. Ask DC Prescott to meet me at the hospital, would you please? Has she given you her new number? ... She has? ... Good.'

Tyrrell arrived at the ITU to find Sarah already waiting for him there, looking drawn and shocked.

'Michael had been moved to the sleep laboratory because of a sudden influx of meningitis cases,' she said, 'and someone switched off the respirator about an hour ago and then locked the door. I've got the nurse who was on duty and the head of the cardiac resuscitation team in the night sister's office and there's a uniformed man guarding the door which was broken down.'

Tyrrell could see that Sarah was close to tears and avoided looking straight at her.

'I'll get on to the scene-of-the-crime men,' he said 'and perhaps you'd impress on the constable not to let anyone in until they arrive.'

After he had finished on the telephone at the nurses' station, Tyrrell saw that both Margaret Melrose and Pentland were in the ITU office and went to have a word with them. Neither of them had much to say, both having been called by the night sister and having arrived after the resuscitation team had given up their attempts to revive Michael.

'Have you contacted Doctor Longley yet?'

'I did ring his house,' Margaret Melrose replied, 'but his wife told me that he was away for the night and she didn't know where.'

'Right, thank you. Please go back to bed if you wish; I'll speak to you both later in the morning.'

The detective met Sarah in the corridor and they walked quickly to the night-sister's office, where the young Australian nurse was waiting.

'Thank you, Sister,' he said briskly, 'we'll be able to manage on our own now. I'll speak to you later.

Claire Garrard inclined her head and limped silently out of the room.

'What's your name?' Tyrrell asked gently, sitting down beside the young night nurse, who had obviously been crying.

'Felicity Bryant. I hadn't left him for more than ten minutes and....'

There was a rising note of hysteria in her voice and Tyrrell assumed his most reassuring manner. 'Steady on,' he said, 'I'm sure you did nothing wrong. You were on duty at the nursing station when it happened, were you?'

The young woman nodded. 'Yes and the other nurses were working in the two other wards, the three-bedded one and the larger one. As well as keeping an eye on the monitors and answering the phone, it was my responsibility to look in on Michael every hour or so.'

'Why not tell me exactly what happened?'

When she had finished her account, the young woman began to cry again and Sarah put her arm around her shoulders.

'I'm sorry,' she said. 'I'm not usually like this, but the whole evening had been winding me up and what happened to Michael was the last straw.'

'What exactly was worrying you?'

'I know I'm only from an agency, but I've had a lot of experience of ITU work and the night sister treated me as if I was a complete novice and not to be trusted.'

'How exactly?'

'If she looked in once, it must have been a dozen times; she seemed much more worried about Michael than any of the other patients and I couldn't understand why. I had been through his notes and there had been no trouble with his care for weeks. He seemed perfectly comfortable in his new bed and whenever I went in to see him and he was awake he always signalled "no" whenever I asked him if he needed anything.'

'The door was obviously locked when you went to help Michael; what was the arrangement about the key?'

'I don't know. It was always left open unless Michael was being washed and never locked when I was on duty and I don't even know where the key was kept.'

'Who would, do you think?'

'The night sister, or Sister Mountfield, I imagine.'

'Apart from Sister Garrard, did anyone else come to see Michael this evening while you were on duty?'

'Doctor Lee did her night round at about ten, but she just enquired about Michael and looked at him on the monitor. She didn't go into the room, though, but he did have one visitor earlier in the evening. It must have been at about eight-thirty, soon after I came on duty.'

'What did he or she look like?'

'He was a slight man with thick, dark hair, who was wearing horn-rimmed glasses.'

'Did he have a clerical collar on by any chance?'

'Now you mention it, yes he did.'

The anaesthetist, who was head of the cardiac-arrest team, had little new to report. He had arrived with his assistant under five minutes from receiving the call; they had the door open within another three and just had time to notice that the respirator had been switched off and that both the alarms were going off, before trying cardiac massage and manual ventilation with oxygen. He knew before he had started that it was too late, but they had made the attempt nonetheless.

'Did you move anything in the room?'

The man raised his eyebrows. 'Well, it's pretty small, there were two of us in there plus the nurse, we also had a trolley and there was a bit of a panic on, so we just pushed everything else out of the way.'

'That I can well understand. Thanks for your help. Please don't stay up; we won't be needing you again tonight.'

The anaesthetist gave him a rueful smile. 'Thank goodness for that.'

Pocock and the scene-of-the-crime were still working in the sleep-study room when Sister Mountfield came on duty and they were able to establish that the key to the door of that room was always left in the lock on the inside of the door so that it could be used to allow Michael privacy when he was being washed or attended to in other ways. The communicating door to the adjacent laboratory and the one from it to the corridor were both kept locked and the keys held by Doctor Leyland.

Tyrrell hesitated for a moment after the sister had left her office, then looked across at Sarah. 'You saw a good deal more of Michael than I did,' he said, 'and I know how upset you must be, but do you feel strong enough to come with me to the sleep-study room directly Pocock has finished?'

'Yes, of course. I was terribly shocked when I first heard the news, but I'm all right now. There's something distinctly odd about all this.'

'In what way?'

'I had a hunch that Michael was on to something when I spoke to him yesterday afternoon and it's obvious that the murderer thought so, too. Poor Michael, I can't help in one way feeling a sense of relief that his ordeal is over at last, but why didn't he tell me what was on his mind? He obviously thought he was in some danger, too; why else was he so insistent that no one else knew about the Morse? And why did Calvert come to see him? As far as I know, he had never done so before.'

They had to wait for another half hour before the scene-of-the-crime team had finished and then Pocock and his assistant took them along to the sleep-study room.

'Did you find him exactly like this?'

The man nodded. 'They'd put a sheet over him after they had failed to resuscitate him.'

Tyrrell turned it back and looked for a few moments at the man they had got to know so well in the preceding few days.

'Is that where those terminals were attached, Sarah?' he asked, bending forward to inspect Donovan's temples, where there were a few flakes of adhesive attached to his skin.

'Yes, you can see the leads hanging down from that box over there.'

'I suppose they must have ripped them off when they tried to resuscitate him. Find anything of interest, Jack?'

'Not really,' the man said lugubriously. 'There were fingerprints all over the place and, according to the sister on duty now, any number of people have been in here and I doubt if we'll learn anything from them.'

'What about that TV camera?'

'It's an infra-red one and, as you can see, it is set high up in the wall opposite the foot of the bed and is angled down so that it took in the head and shoulders of the man lying in the bed. It is unfortunate that the pictures were not being recorded because the socket in the wall, containing the plug for the ventilator, which you can see down there on the right of the bed as you look at it from the direction the camera is pointing, is clearly visible on the monitor.'

'Hmm. Allowing for the fact that it took the nurse a little time to react, she must have been at the door there within a minute or so of the alarm going off.'

'Ample time for whoever operated the switch to get away.'

'What? To lock the door and disappear?'

'Yes. I can't exactly replicate what happened because the door is smashed up, but why not go to the nursing station and keep your eyes on the monitor and when Tom here switches on the alarm on the ventilator, get back as quickly as you can. There's a stopwatch here and you can time it.'

The two detectives followed his suggestion and quite clearly on the monitor, they could see the shape of the upper part of Michael's body and on the side wall by the bed, the socket into which the ventilator was plugged in. As they watched, they saw the end of a rod appear, the switch was turned off and at the same time the alarm sounded. Sarah, who had been sitting in the exact spot where the nurse had been, looked up at the screen and then pushed back the chair and ran out of the station and along the corridor, with Tyrrell following and holding the stop watch. When she reached the door, Jack Pocock appeared from round the right angle bend of the corridor just beyond.

'Hmm,' said Tyrrell, 'about thirty seconds and I reckon, considering that we were expecting it, the nurse would have been rather slower. What exactly did you do, Jack?'

'As you probably noticed, the door opens outwards and is very wide, no doubt to allow easier access for equipment, and I squatted down near it, out of sight of the camera, pushing the switch with my telescopic rod here. Then, allowing a little time pretending to close and lock the door, I nipped round the corner out of sight of the corridor along which you were coming.'

'What's round there?'

'The lifts and staircase'

'I'm convinced. Good work, Jack.'

CHAPTER THIRTEEN

There was a café that served breakfast a few hundred yards up the road from the hospital, but neither of the two detectives had much appetite.

'It certainly looks as if the murderer had quite a knowledge of both respirators and the set-up in that sleep-study room,' Tyrrell said, as he sipped his second cup of coffee.

'Yes, and it surely must have been someone who was in the chapel on both occasions.'

'That's right and we can narrow it down further to those who had access to the table behind Michael's bed, but that still leaves us with Doctors Longley, Melrose, Pentland, and Lee, the nurses Claire Garrard and Liz Fletcher and the physiotherapist Jacquie.'

'We can eliminate Doctor Melrose. Her flat is at least twenty minutes' drive away, even in the middle of the night, and she was at home when the night sister gave her a ring only some ten minutes after Michael was killed.'

'I agree with that. As far as the rest of them are concerned, Pentland says he was asleep in his room, as did Doctor Lee, but either of them would have had ample time to get back there before they were called and so far Longley can't be traced. Claire Garrard claims to have been in her office until her bleep went, but not only was there no one to corroborate that, but she could easily have nipped back there – it's only a couple of minutes from the ITU. I must say that I can't see either Jacquie or Liz being responsible, but we'll need to check up on both of them and Longley as soon as he gets into work.'

'Perhaps we ought to have a word with the night porter as well. I can't imagine that more than an absolute minimum of entrances is kept open at night and he might have seen one of those people. Obviously one would have expected Sister Garrard to have been wandering around the place, but that wouldn't have been true of any of the others, particularly as we know that there weren't any emergency calls from the ITU until the agency nurse sent for the cardiac-arrest team.'

Tyrrell made a note on the pad beside him and then glanced at his watch.

Although it was only 8.30 by the time the two detectives got back to the hospital, the night porter had already left and Clifford Longley's secretary was at her desk and gave them a bright smile when they came into the office.

'Doctor Longley's expecting you,' she said. 'I'll let him know that you're here.'

The physician was standing behind his desk when they were shown in and he motioned them to sit down.

'I didn't believe it when you told me you thought that someone here had killed Father Carey, but I do now.'

'When did you hear about Michael?'

'Doctor Melrose left a note for me in my pigeon-hole in the front hall and I found it when I arrived here at eight. Naturally I went straight to the unit and I've only just got back here. This whole business is dreadful thing for the hospital and it's even worse to think that there's a murderer in our midst, but I can only feel relief that

Michael had been freed from his long ordeal. He was an intelligent man and knew perfectly well that he had no hope of improvement in his condition and if it had been me, I would certainly have wanted to die. Keeping patients such as him going is a very serious dilemma for all of us. At the beginning, when there is a chance of substantial improvement or even of recovery, there is clearly no choice but to do one's utmost to ensure survival, but later on.... A few years back, we used to turn respirators off; it was done quietly and discreetly and relatives were quite happy in their belief that the patient had died of a "heart attack", but now it's quite a different matter. We've been overtaken by rules about brain death, ill-informed talk about misdiagnoses and the fear of litigation and we have become prisoners of technology.'

The man suddenly seemed to realize that he had been talking too much and Tyrrell sensed that a lot of his previous self-confidence had evaporated.

'Michael Donovan was killed very soon after two a.m.' Tyrrell paused long enough to make the silence awkward. 'I wonder if you would be good enough to tell me where you were at that time.'

The answer came back without any hesitation. 'I took Sharon to the new Lloyd Webber musical, we then had supper, went dancing at Gavroni's and spent the night together at the Roskill Hotel.'

'And at two a.m?'

'We were in bed.' Longley took out his wallet, extracted a credit-card receipt and handed it across the desk. 'I paid the hotel with this and no doubt the night porter will remember letting us in.'

'What time did you get there?'

'At about one o'clock.'

'And Sharon was with you all the time?'

'Yes, she was.'

'And no doubt she'll be able to confirm it?'

'Are you suggesting that I crept out of the hotel when she was asleep, murdered Donovan, and then returned there, all without being seen?'

'I'm not suggesting anything, merely trying to eliminate you from our enquiries.'

'All right, I suppose you'd better have a word with her.'

'Would it make it easier if my colleague here did so?'

'I think it would.' Longley pressed the buzzer on his desk. 'Ah, Sharon,' he said, when she came in, 'one of our patients died under suspicious circumstances at about two a.m. last night and Chief Inspector Tyrrell and his assistant here would like to know the whereabouts of all the people who were concerned with his management here. I'd like you to tell DC Prescott what we were doing last night and where we were doing it and, what's more, I don't wish you to hold back anything, anything at all. Is that clear?'

The young woman looked at him very directly for a moment or two and then at Sarah, a faint flush on her cheeks.

'Don't worry, just tell her the truth I've been assured that it won't go any further.' Tyrrell hadn't done any such thing, but when the girl glanced at him, he nodded. 'Right, might I suggest that you use this office and the chief inspector and I will deal with the phone next door to ensure that you're not disturbed.'

Sarah studiously avoided looking at her superior as they went down to the front hall some fifteen minutes later.

'It was exactly as he'd said. They went to that musical

followed by the night club and were at the hotel at about one a.m.'

'And then?'

'There was no way that Longley could have gone back to the hospital by two.'

'Why not?'

'For one thing Sharon was wide awake until much later than that and for another, he was tied up for the rest of the night – quite literally, I mean. Longley likes to try out all the variations and it was Sharon's turn to take the initiative. They run to four-poster beds at the Roskill and she used the uprights to secure him. She told me that he couldn't have got loose even if he'd wanted to and he didn't. Do you want me to go on?'

Tyrrell gave her a wry smile. 'I'll spare your blushes for the moment. I must say this for Longley, one has to admire his stamina – he looks as fresh as paint this morning. I suppose, though, that we have to consider the possibility that he cooked up that story and bribed Sharon to confirm it. If he did do that, though, he went to some lengths – I happened to notice some quite nasty abrasions on his wrists when he stretched his arm out to press that buzzer. What did you make of her?'

'I got the impression that she still hasn't quite taken in what's hit her in her relationship with Longley. As far as she's concerned, it's all been something of a fairy tale; you see, if she has a fantasy, she only has to mention it and he presses the button and makes it happen. Evidently he told her to plan yesterday evening in any way she liked and he'd foot the bill.'

'So the bondage bit was her idea?'

'That's what she said.'

'And did you believe her?'

'Yes, incredible though it may seem, I did. It appears that they take it turn and turn about to devise things to do and what games to play. I did wonder why she was so ready with all the intimate details and hinted as much to her and she came straight out with the fact that he'd told her not to hold anything back and that she always did exactly what he asked of her. I think she worships the ground he walks on.'

'What a dull life I've led.' He smiled. 'I wouldn't want to swap with what I've got, though, would you?'

Sarah was fairly sure that Tyrrell wasn't expecting an answer, at least she hoped not, because she certainly wasn't going to give him one. She had found Sharon's description of what she and Longley had got up to highly disturbing and the thought that it had actually happened, made it much more arousing than any of the stories she had read furtively in the soft-core porn magazines that some of the men had left lying around during her training course.

'Well, perhaps we ought to call on Calvert next; it seems more than a bit strange that he should have been to see Michael for the first time last night of all nights.'

'Excuse me, sir.'

Tyrrell, who had been on the point of dialling the chaplain's number on the internal telephone on the counter in the front hall, turned to see the porter they had met previously, who had come out of the room immediately behind it.

'Doctor Leyland would like to see you urgently, sir.'

'Doctor Leyland?'

'He's the research registrar in clinical neurophysiology. He said that if I gave him a ring, he'd come up right away.'

'Did he say what he wanted?'

'No, sir, just that it was very important.'

Colin Leyland was a brisk young man with ginger hair, who came bounding up the staircase leading from the basement.

'Last night,' he said, when he had introduced himself, 'Michael Donovan asked me to give you something; he said that there wasn't any particular hurry, but when I arrived this morning and heard what had happened to him during the night, I thought I'd better contact you as soon as possible and Sister Mountfield told me you were here somewhere, hence my message with the porter.'

'What was it he wanted me to have?'

'It would be easier to explain and give it to you down in my lab.'

'Lead the way.'

The laboratory was a clutter of monitors, amplifiers and other pieces of apparatus and the registrar had to move several piles of paper recordings off two of the chairs to give them both seats.

'I'm in charge of the sleep laboratory and EEG telemetry service and I can tell you that I wasn't best pleased when they told me that Michael Donovan would have to go into the telemetry room for the duration of the meningitis flap. It meant cancelling all the studies I had planned and also moving all the portable equipment down here. With the door having to be left open, it would have walked within a matter of hours, but at least I was able to secure the adjacent lab. Anyway, after Michael was moved, I got talking to him and was explaining to him what I was working on and was watching his "yes" and "no" responses when I realized that it would be possible to record them.'

'In what way?'

'Well, not only are blinks easy to record, but they

generate quite large electrical impulses and I thought it might be possible for him to operate some switching gear with them to turn his TV or cassette recorder on and off. I was explaining that to him when he suddenly started to produce a pattern of blinks that I recognized as SOS. To cut a long story short, within half an hour I was able to put his short and long blinks on to a paper recorder, I got hold of the Morse Code off the internet and was then able to read and translate his messages. I must say it seems to me quite incredible that no one here thought of doing that before – the poor fellow was in the unit for six months and during all that time all he was able to do was signal "yes" and "no".'

'Were those electrodes attached to his temples to do with your recording?'

'Yes, that's right. As I told you, the voltages are large and don't require much amplification and the whole exercise was simplicity itself; I plugged the leads into a junction box in the lab next door and they were cabled down here and on to the big paper recorder over there. As I told Michael, it runs for eight hours and he could record a book on it if he wanted to.'

'What was his reaction?'

'Excitement. He asked me particularly not to tell a soul about it as he wanted it to be a surprise to everyone when he had perfected his technique.'

'Was he able to communicate with you direct?'

'Not really, apart from the "yes" and "no". I didn't have time to learn the code properly and found it easier to record the dots and dashes and convert them then.'

'Did Michael ask you to do anything else?'

'Yes. Firstly, he wanted to make a will. He used to be a solicitor and thought that if I were to type it out, read it to him, then impress his forefinger print on some sealing wax and then witness it myself, it should be valid. Then, when I was satisfied that recordings during the night would work properly on the timer I had rigged up, he requested me to set up the eight-hour tape last night starting at ten o'clock. Finally, he asked me to get Father Calvert to come to see him no earlier than that.'

'Father Calvert? Did he say why?'

'Yes. Donovan told me that Father Carey had been particularly kind to him and he wanted to talk to another priest, who also happened to be the man's best friend.'

'How did he propose to do that?'

'He asked me to explain to him how I had discovered about the Morse and to give him a copy of the code. Oh, and he said that I was to tell him that I had only found out about it that morning and that he didn't want Calvert to know about the recording.'

'Did he say why?'

'No, just that it was most important and that he would explain the reasons later.'

'What was Calvert's reaction?'

'He said that he would be only too pleased to do what he could to help and he understood how hard Father Carey's death must have hit him. There was one other thing, too.'

'Which was?'

'Michael asked me if it would be possible to make a video recording from the camera on the opposite wall to run at the same time.'

'And was it?'

'Yes, quite simple, in fact. It's already set up for the sleep and epilepsy studies and I only had to switch the timer on.'

'Did he say why he wanted you to do that as well?'

'No, he didn't; he just asked me to give both the records to you this morning, unless he said anything to the contrary to me when I came in.'

'Have you seen or read either of them?'

'No. Not only did he ask me not to as it would contain a lot of personal things, but it would have taken me not hours but days – there are reams of the stuff.' He pointed to the enormous reel on the spool. 'What should make it easier for your people is that I suggested that he should sign on and off by using five dots in order not to adulterate the tape with random blinks, which of course will have been recorded as well. There is one more thing and that is his will, which I typed out and read to him a couple of days ago. I've signed it and it has the print of his right index finger on the seal on it. It is in this envelope and he did say that he was most anxious that you should read it before anyone else.'

He handed it across to Tyrrell, who nodded, put it in the breast pocket of his jacket and after he had thanked the young man and arranged for the tapes to be dispatched to the Yard, he rang Father Calvert, who met them in his rooms.

'I blame myself terribly, he said, shaking his head when he was told about Donovan's death.

'In what way?'

'One of the doctors, a fellow called Leyland, came to see me yesterday afternoon to say that he had only discovered that morning that Donovan knew the Morse Code and was able to transmit it by means of eye blinks. He asked me if I would go up to see him early that evening as he had something special he wanted to communicate to me.'

'And you did go up there?'

'Yes, I did, and although I already had a working knowledge of Morse, it took me took me some time to work out what he wanted to say.'

'And it was?'

'That he knew who had killed Patrick.' He looked directly at both of them in turn. 'I'm not sure that I should be telling you this – it is only hearsay.'

'We realize that.'

'He told me that when Sister Garrard was asked to go behind his bed in the chapel during that reconstruction, he picked up a faint smell of what he thought was iodine. He said that since his accident his sense of smell had become very acute and that he was sure that it was the same one he had noticed when he heard Patrick's hip flask being moved during the Mass.'

'Why do you suppose he told you this rather than us?'

'I think it must have been because he hadn't been able to communicate with anyone properly before yesterday and needed time to work out what he should do. He found himself in a terrible dilemma; he realized that the evidence was flimsy and didn't want to cast suspicion on her unfairly, but on the other hand he knew that it might be just the clue you were looking for. I suppose he thought that a priest might be able to help him over his decision.'

'What was your advice?'

'I said I wanted to sleep on it and that I would come to see him again today. I obviously should have rung you about it straight away and then you'd have been able to put a guard on him – I'll never forgive myself.'

'In your shoes, I would probably have done exactly the same thing. What is your own view about Michael's suspicions?'

'I had doubts about even telling you this much and I

couldn't possibly speculate about someone I've not even met.'

'Did anyone apart from Leyland know that you were going to see Michael?'

'No, but naturally I reported to the nurse on duty – I couldn't have gone barging in there without asking permission. I suppose others might have seen that I was in there – I was with him for a good half-hour.'

After they had left the chaplain, the two detectives made their way slowly back to the front hall.

'What do you make of all that, Sarah?'

'I don't understand it at all. Why didn't Michael tell us about the smell of iodine and having heard the hip flask being moved? He had ample opportunity to do so and why confide in someone he didn't even know? He was up to something, I have no doubt of it.'

'I wouldn't be quite so certain. He was suspicious of Claire Garrard, but he may well have had doubts about condemning her merely on his sense of smell. While we're on the subject, why don't we have a word with one of the pharmacists? I thought iodine went out with the Crimean War.'

The chief pharmacist was a tall, soft-spoken Sikh, who seemed to find nothing strange about Tyrrell's query.

'Iodine preparations are still used a great deal here, particularly by the operating staff. It is strongly bactericidal and is used both for scrubbing up and in the skin preparation of the patient before surgery.'

'Does the preparation they use here have a strong smell?'

'Not particularly.'

He walked across to one of the shelves, reached for a bottle and after unscrewing the top handed it across to the detectives.

'And it's freely available around the hospital?'

'Oh yes, particularly since the concern about MRSA; you'll find some on all the wards.'

Sarah gave Tyrrell a rueful smile when he looked at her when they were back in the corridor. 'I suppose you want me to see if Claire Garrard smells of iodine.'

'How did you guess? Why not ask her if she saw anyone unusual hanging around the ITU when she was doing her rounds last night? That'll be a good enough excuse for going to see her. For the time being, though, I don't think we should do anything else until we've seen what Michael put on those recordings. I'll wait for you in the car.'

Sarah reappeared ten minutes later and slipped into the passenger seat beside him.

'And does she?'

She nodded. 'And, what's more, she's got a bottle of the stuff in her bathroom – I pretended to have urgent need of the facilities.'

'Hmm. How did she strike you this morning?'

'Her emotions were under strict control and she had nothing to add.'

Tyrrell rubbed his chin reflectively. 'I'm going back home for a bath and a shave; care to come with me? You might like to have a bite of lunch and lie down for an hour or two; they're going to deliver the transcript of that tape there, but I've just been on the phone to them and they don't expect it to be ready until the late afternoon at the earliest.'

'Will your wife be able to put up with me?'

'I'm sure she'll be only too delighted; she was saying only the other day how keen she was to meet you.'

'I'd like to very much, then.'

'Splendid. Oh, Sarah!'

There was something in his tone of voice that made her look up at him and she saw that he was staring straight ahead through the windscreen.

'Yes.'

'While you were with Claire Garrard, I had a look at the will that Leyland typed out for Michael. He's left you his flat in Putney. It's on a long lease and he's given instructions that the mortgage is to be paid off from the residue of his estate.'

The transcript arrived just after six o'clock and they both settled down to read it, Tyrrell passing across each page after he had finished it.

This is my chance. Leyland is a godsend; he is quick, reliable and intelligent and, most important of all, has no idea of what is going on. He also seems genuinely upset that the doctors haven't made more effort to communicate with me, which is why I believe that he will carry out my instructions to the letter. I sense that he can't understand why I wanted him to tell Calvert about the Morse, but at the same time was adamant about his being kept in the dark about my blinks being recorded. I said I'd explain later, which seemed to keep him reasonably happy.

Why am I so sure that it was Calvert? It was his expensive aftershave lotion that did it – one of the forwards in our rugby team also used the same make. I smelled it coming from behind the bed when Patrick was delivering his sermon and again when Calvert came out of the vestry yesterday. You'll have to check, but someone hiding in the vestry with the door open just a little, would probably have had no difficulty in reaching for the flask on the table, putting the poison in and then replacing it. The flower vase, my bed and the door would all have helped to hide what he was doing. It seems likely that he came into the vestry through the door at the back of the broom cupboard in the corridor outside – I'll leave you to work that one out.

Why did he do it? I've spent hours wondering. He wouldn't have gone into the vestry on the off chance and that means he must have known about the hip flask. I'd forgotten until now, but I remember Patrick telling me that he always left it there during the Mass. If he did, which seems more likely than a chance discovery on another occasion, it implies an intimate friendship. How intimate? I think Patrick must have been homosexual. He dropped hints about it to me on more than one occasion and could infidelity, jealousy, or a lover's quarrel have been the motive? There's no way I can think of to prove all this, which is why I want to see Calvert and provoke him into doing something else. Let us hope that killing two birds with one stone will be the literal truth – this particular bird has had enough. First of all, though, he'll have to come and....

At that point, Donovan signed off and the transcriber noted that there had been a gap of just under forty-five minutes before he signalled that he was ready to transmit again.

I can hear someone at the door and I'll describe what happened later.

There was a further pause of just over half an hour before the five dots appeared again.

You'll have a record of my side of the conversation, but I'll go over it again. He was introduced by the nurse and then stood looking at me intently.

'What can I do for you?' he asked, the aftershave lotion as evident as before.

It was a laborious business because he had to write down the dots and dashes and then transcribe them using the sheet of paper with the Morse written on it that Leyland had given him.

'You killed Patrick,' I signalled.

He's no fool, this Calvert, and I could see him looking round the room and up at the camera and the microphone beside it.

'What do you mean?' he whispered right in my ear.

'I have proof.'

'What proof?'

'Your aftershave lotion, amongst other things.'

'Why are you telling me this?'

'To give you the opportunity to confess to the detective.'

'Have you told him about this yourself?'

'Not yet. My ability to transmit Morse was only discovered by Doctor Leyland today.'

It sounded pretty thin to me, but would he take the bait? Only time will tell – I can hear him moving about – and then he left without saying another word. All I can do now is hope for the best.

There was then a very long gap until just after two a.m., when Donovan began to signal again.

He's here – I can smell the lotion again. The main light is out, but I can seen occasional flashes from a shaded torch.

The transcriber indicated that the speed of transmission had accelerated greatly.

I think he's crawling by the side of the bed. Yes, I heard the click of the switch by the plug and the ventilator's stopped. The alarm on it is sounding and I hear hurried footsteps and the door being locked. So that's how he decided to do it. Feeling tight in the chest and dizzy, but quite calm. Thank you, Roger, for all your kindness and to the doctors and nurses. Special thanks and love to you, Sarah. In other circumstances, we might have ... find someone to....

Tyrrell put the sheet he had just finished down on the occasional table beside the armchair in which Sarah was sitting and got to his feet.

'Just going to see how supper's getting on,' he said, slipping out through the door.

Alison was stirring a saucepan on the top of the cooker and turned round when she heard him at the door.

'What's wrong, love?'

'It's Sarah. I'm worried about her.'

He gave her a summary of the transcript, in particular what Michael had transmitted in the minute or two before he had died, and also told her about the will he had made.

'I thought it best to leave her on her own while she read the last page. You see, I think that Michael genuinely fell in love with her – she spent quite a long time with him alone – and without wanting to romanticize it, I'm quite sure that she felt the same way about him. It isn't that she told me anything about it, but I saw the way she looked at him and held his hand and I wish to God I'd said something when I first noticed it. You see, Sarah had an unhappy and very sheltered upbringing and to make matters worse, she was lucky to have escaped being raped recently. All that means that that not only has she not had the opportunity to gain any experience with men, but she's bound to be particularly sensitive to anything like that just now. She was obviously terribly upset by Michael's death, as I was, but she appeared to get over it remarkably quickly: I have a feeling, though, that reading that transcript is going to prove pretty devastating, not to mention his will.'

'Would you like me to go to her?'

'Would you?'

Alison lifted the saucepan away from the burner and gave him a hug.

'Of course. Look after this, would you? There are also some carrots and potatoes to peel and put on if you feel strong enough.'

'You won't say anything about the attempted rape unless she brings it up herself, will you? When she told me about it, I did promise that it would be just between the two of us – it was someone at work, you see.'

Alison never did tell him what had happened in the sitting-room and he didn't ask, but nearly an hour went by before she came back into the kitchen, looking red around the eyes herself.

'She's all right now.'

'Will she be able to face supper?'

'I think so. Mandy came down a few minutes ago – trouble with her homework, yet again. Sarah volunteered to help her.'

'And if that doesn't cheer her up, nothing will.'

'That's enough of the sarcasm. You haven't seen your daughter in action as often as I have – she's even been known to cheer your mother up.'

She neatly caught the dish cloth which had come sailing through the air in her direction.

'How about laying the table?'

Alison was right, as usual, he thought. When he went into the sitting-room ten minutes later to tell them that the meal was ready, Mandy and Sarah were having an animated discussion about the relative merits of various makes and styles of jeans and the girl kept up a continuous flow of chatter throughout supper, completely undeterred by her brother Timothy's attempt to shut her up.

CHAPTER FOURTEEN

Sarah's mouth was dry and her heart was pounding as Calvert showed them into the living-room of his flat, which had a separate entrance in the area beneath the nurses' hostel, but Tyrrell seemed as relaxed and urbane as usual as he sat down in one of the easy chairs, one long leg crossed over the other.

'Would either of you care for a cup of coffee?'

'No, thank you.'

'What can I do for you this time?'

'We'd just like to know why you did it.'

Calvert's expression didn't alter and he continued to look straight at the detective through his glasses.

'I don't understand you.'

'You poisoned Patrick Carey by putting an extract of *amanita phalloides* into his whiskey flask. The lock on the second door to the vestry from the store cupboard off the corridor has been lubricated recently with graphite and you went in there that way during the Mass for Michael Donovan. You were no doubt surprised to find that the hip flask wasn't in its usual place in the vestry, but when you glanced through the door which was open a crack, you saw it on the table by the flower vase and that it was reachable by your outstretched arm. It was then that Michael caught the scent of your aftershave lotion, but he didn't realize the full significance of it until the reconstruction in the chapel when he smelled it again when you came out of the vestry. How do we know all this? Michael's blinks were recorded on Doctor Leyland's apparatus last night and we had it transcribed. The rubber sheath on the end of that rather elegant walking stick of yours, which I noticed in the stand just inside your front door, was also seen when you switched the respirator off with it.'

'Seen? How?'

'Infra-red cameras work efficiently in low background illumination, as I'm sure you know, and the pictures from it were also recorded.'

The man failed to react for a moment, but when Tyrrell started to caution him, he bent forward slightly and put his hand to his chest.

'My heart. It plays me up rather from time to time, particularly at times of stress.'

Calvert got to his feet, walked very slowly across to the cupboard set into the angle of the walls and reached out for the bottle of medicine with a plastic cup resting on top of it. He poured out a generous measure, swallowed it in one gulp, then returned to his seat.

'You'll forgive me, I hope, if I take my time. I've not been at all well for the last few days and I wouldn't want anything to happen to me before I've finished trying to explain it all to you.'

His voice had become much softer, such that the two of them had to strain to hear him, and it was almost devoid of expression.

'Patrick and I were very happy until he acquired all that money. He was a terrible gambler, was Patrick, the horses, the dogs, the pools, in fact, anything you care to mention, but it never did any great harm because he never won very much and he had precious little to lose. Curiously, it wasn't even proper gambling that brought him the jackpot – he won one of the top prizes with one of the very few premium bonds he held – and it was that that ruined everything.

'I knew, of course, that he had unusual sexual fantasies and impulses of a sadistic nature; I never dreamt that he would either want to, or be able to put them into practice. It was when he was drunk one Thursday evening, too drunk to be able to play chess, that he told me about the money and the photographs that you no doubt found in the presbytery. I don't think he would have done so had I not been going on at him about the drink; we had a silly row and I suppose he did it to spite me. I was quite devastated; I was hurt, I was jealous and I was angry. I was not only angry, I was also afraid; some of those boys were drug addicts and not only was Patrick putting me at risk from the mundane venereal infections, but also AIDS. Later on, he was full of remorse and protestations that it would never happen again and I was taken in for a time, but then, after I had kept a watch on the presbytery, I saw that he hadn't meant a word of it. My love turned to hate and one doesn't behave rationally if one is in love with or hates someone.

'What I did was quite calculated. I am not a violent person and even though when I planned it all I was more than a little mad, I knew that I would never be able to kill him using force and it had to be poison. Why amanita phalloides? It was partly because Patrick disliked mushroms so much and partly because they were available and untraceable, but the main reason was that he had told me that Claire Garrard had once worked on a mushroom farm. He also told me a very great deal more about her than that. I've never spoken a single word to her myself, but Patrick had an absolute obsession about the woman and after the hours he had spent talking about her in his more bibulous moments, I came to believe that I knew her almost as well as he did and that I had been her confessor, not him. Do you know, I almost came to believe that she was the one to have done the poisoning?

'She was the perfect suspect, should it be discovered that Patrick's death was not due to natural causes. She was, after all, a woman with many secrets, who had come to believe, despite his denials to the contrary, that Patrick wouldn't keep them and if he didn't, then her future in the hospital would be jeopardized. In fact, she was convinced that he had already spoken out of turn and she was right; he had, after all, told me and I had a shrewd suspicion that others might well have picked up the same information as a result of one of his indiscretions. She had a good deal to hide, too; she had been a nun, had masochistic tendencies and had been consoled by one of the senior physicians. She is clearly no fool that Claire Garrard, and must have either guessed or been told that Patrick was gay. At any rate, she may in the beginning have been the subservient nun confessing to a priest, but later on, Patrick told me that she had attacked him for drinking, for breaking his vows of chastity and for his AIDS campaign. Oh yes, she had good reason to hate him and so easily might have decided to kill him.

'That mass for Donovan was the perfect opportunity for me. Patrick always left his flask in the vestry while he was saying Mass – he forgot to pick it up once and told me about it – and I was able to slip in through the back door from the cleaning place without any real risk of being seen.

As you guessed, I was taken aback when I failed to find it there, but the when I saw it on the table through the half-open door, I realized that that would make the whole thing even better. Any number of people would have had easy access to it.

'Why did I kill Michael Donovan as well? I think the honest answer is that I still wanted to save my skin and I also managed to convince myself that I would be doing him a service. The man wanted to die – Patrick told me that any number of times – and Donovan as good as asked me to do it when he told me that he knew that I'd killed Patrick. I couldn't think of any other reason why he hadn't gone to you first. Patrick had also told me that Claire Garrard was forever washing her hands with iodine scrub because fear of AIDS and MRSA was another of her obsessions and it was during your reconstruction in the chapel that I picked up the smell of it. That's what gave me the idea of telling you about it after Donovan had said that it was my aftershave lotion that had given me away. You see, even at that late stage, it was almost as if I was denying to myself what I had done.'

Calvert got to his feet and walked slowly towards the window and stood looking out. 'Michael Donovan,' he said, 'couldn't bear the thought of remaining imprisoned by his respirator any more than I can of being stuck in a prison cell for years or even the rest of my life. He had the courage and ingenuity to do something about it and so have I. Poetic justice, don't you think?'

'*Amanita phalloides* in your "medicine"?'

'You're clearly no fool, Tyrrell. If you guessed what I was doing at the time, then I am in your debt, because you might have stopped me, or even tried to make me bring the poison up, but if you didn't, then you've missed the boat – I'm quite sure it's too late to do anything about it now.' He turned to face them. 'I'm ready to go with you now.'